HOOKING UP WITH NUMBER 36

THE SIN BIN SERIES

EDEN KNOX

For all the good girls.
Daddy Bishop said to drink your water.

CONTENT WARNING

This book contains matter that some readers may find uncomfortable. Explicit sexual encounters are present. The characters participate in anonymous, "hook up" sexual relationships. There are situations of Dom/sub play with mention of bondage/shibari.

Reader discretion is advised.

CHAPTER 1
BISHOP

OF ALL THE clubs in the metro area, she just had to walk into Caissa. The one with a VIP, members only sex club in the back. Mine.

No one really knows that it's my club, or that I designed it this way. Fun dance club in the front, general admission, white fixtures everywhere. In the back is a bouncer for entry to another club, membership only, and very exclusive. Caissa, the goddess of Chess, the black and white design, it's my backup plan for retirement. I'm sure there's some kind of symbolism for protecting my livelihood and the strategies at play here, but I can't be bothered to delve into that.

I feel her gaze travel from the top of my dark waves I have pulled back into a ponytail, down to the silver wolf's mask I wore for the masquerade party. Her eyes slowly roam down my bespoke suit to my Italian leather shoes. The weight of her appraisal excites me, my heart racing, just like when a player is screaming toward me on a breakaway. I will never get tired of this, I love the burst of endorphins it gives me. My outfit is impeccable, as always, but all I get from her emerald gaze is a casual perusal. Her eyes stay locked on me for two heartbeats before she's looking elsewhere, taking in the caged performers around the room. Our connection breaks, and I'm left with a startling realization: I fall short of her expectations. Me, of all people. I'm Valentin Mother-Fucking Bishop, and I'm a damn hockey God. Women want me, men want to be me, this doesn't happen. I don't get blown off like this.

Fucking brat.

I sit back against the rich black curtains draped along the walls and take her in, watching her move toward the small bar to pick up a martini glass of something red, and then searching out the crowd. Her white glowing wristband catches my eye—she has to be new here in order to get one of those, but is moving around the room with the comfort of a regular member.

To members of Caissa, white wristbands mean different things to different people. Some would see it and proceed with caution—the person is uninitiated into the proprietary nature of my private club. To others, it means there's fresh blood on the dance floor which, unfortunately, can draw in the sharks. Red bands are for newer members, as they are prone to overexcitement and need correction frequently, reminded what safe play means. Caissa has a code of conduct, and the first rule: No touching without consent. Being the silent partner behind the club, it's my duty to make sure behavior within these walls is beyond reproach.

Who is this girl?

Stopping near one of the glossy black-and-white checkered high-top tables on the edge of the dance floor, she sets down a small clutch before turning her gaze longingly toward the entrance. Her brows draw together as she watches someone enter before twisting her heel in a nervous twitch. She looks like she could own this place, but her nervousness breaks the illusion. I can't stop myself from looking at her, the way her dark hair falls in a curtain over her shoulder, the little black dress clinging to her curves, the red-bottomed heels with a black strap wrapping around her ankle. I usually fucking hate the color red, but maybe I'll make an exception for her.

I idly twist my band, the solid-black titanium establishing me as an exclusive member. As a black band, I have a responsibility to watch out for newer members and guide them with my expertise, including protecting white band new members from over-eager red band members.

I make eye contact with a bartender, flashing two fingers in a wave in his direction. He returns my wave with a nod of understanding; prep my drink order, two fingers of my favorite whiskey.

Stepping away from the shadows, I approach her slowly, greeting other guests to not make it obvious I'm coming straight for the newest person in the room. A tall and relatively good-looking blond man walks up to the table from behind her. His red band stands out like the caution flag it's meant to be in here. My steps stutter. I'm not as close to her as he is, so I can't block his approach. Her shoulders stiffen under the thick straps of her little black dress as he presses his hand to her lower back. My jaw aches as I grind my teeth, anger flaring through me. The bastard scared her. I try to tell myself that the surge of anger I feel is just instinctual, it's my responsibility to make sure my guests are safe, and not something ridiculous like jealousy because some dude is near a woman who interests me.

I continue moving toward her, swiping my whiskey from the bar top, then ease close enough that I can listen in to their conversation over the throbbing bass of the dance music.

"Come on, we should go play, sweet thing. You won't regret it."

I roll my eyes at his cheesy pick-up line, but before I can speak up, her sharp voice cuts in leaving no room for argument, "I'm good right where I'm at, thanks." I can't help but smile as she shuts him down faster than I could blink.

Impressive.

"Don't be like that, Duchess." He spits out the name with a tone I don't like, twisting the pet name into an insult. "I should show you just how good things are here," he counters, clearly missing the warning signs of her disinterest. Also, 'should' instead of 'could' is a choice in words that has my jaw clenching.

"I said no," she bites back, making me bristle. He isn't accepting her rejection. That's it. He's gone. I make eye contact with security, point at the douchebag, then walk up to them.

I set my glass on the table, hard enough that the clink of the crystal against the wood makes them startle. The amber liquid sloshing to the rim with the force, leaving a track down the outside of my glass. The fucker spots my wristband. With his spine straightening and head bowed, he mutters, "Sorry," before turning away from us in defeat. Oh, so he knows what the wristband means, but not when he's told no. I hate this guy even more now.

"Not so fast." He pauses at my command. "I think you should apologize to her first."

"I said I was sorry," he protests. I shoot him a dark look, and he finally glances her way. "Okay, sorry, it won't happen again," he growls, throwing me a middle finger before walking away.

"That's better. Good boy," I call after him. Turning back to the captivating woman in front of me, I flash my trademark smile that'll make any woman's panties instantly wet. "My apologies. That behavior isn't allowed here."

"Thank you." Her shoulders sag with relief as she smiles back at me. "He really didn't seem to get that 'no' is a full sentence."

Her freshly manicured nails glint in the flashing lights as she wordlessly reaches for a handshake. I gently take it in mine, flipping it palm down and lifting it to place a kiss between her knuckles. She gasps in surprise, and I wink, smirking at her flustered state.

So fucking adorable. I wonder how far that pretty blush will go, if she'll let me play. *Slow down, Bishop,* I tell myself.

I can be a gentleman when I want to. It all depends on the conversation and the company. "I don't think I've seen you here before," I muse, picking up my tumbler. "Is this your first visit to Caissa?"

"Oh, you come here often, then?" She counters teasingly, sipping her drink while dropping a sideways glance at me. I'm intrigued by her slightly suspicious tone, maybe a touch judgmental.

I reply, "Often enough," I respond vaguely, and take a slow drink of my whiskey. "Someone has to take care of the place and make sure our patrons are happy." I glance over at the asshole who bothered her earlier. "Often enough that I know he would've never worked out for you." I curse internally, hoping she doesn't make too much out of the "our patrons" line, but she seems unfazed by the remark. I relax a bit, hoping she doesn't dig into it too much.

My mystery girl tucks her dark strands behind her ear, the light catching on the jewelry in her lobe. Silver coils—almost like twisted, knotted rope—loop in and around her ear through several piercings. It's subtle but alluring, and I want to know more.

Who is this girl?

"Oh yeah? Please tell me how that would've played out," she tuts, and I'm helplessly drawn to her fire.

"He would have taken you to one of the cheaper rooms." I point out a hallway behind me. "Or simply dragged you into the bathroom for a quick fuck, leaving you completely unsatisfied after the most mediocre sex of your life."

With a smirk, her eyes meet mine as she dares to ask, "And what makes you think I couldn't make it better on my own? I know better than to depend on someone I just met to satisfy me."

"You shouldn't have to work for it, Duchess."

"*Duchess?* I have a real name, and it's not whatever Chad called me."

"I know. But we are all so much more complicated than our names. The title fits you, I think."

"Wow. Does that line work on all the ladies?"

I shrug off her comment. "Besides, I've seen his type in action before. Two, maybe three pumps, and he'll be done, telling you that you're the best he's ever had."

"Maybe I am. But it's not like either of you will find out." She looks away, scanning the crowd again. "It's been fun, but I'm calling it a night. Thanks for the save." She snatches her clutch on the table, but before she can move away from me, I instinctively grip her wrist.

"Not so fast, I have a proposal for you."

Her lips quirk up as she looks me up and down one more time. "And what's that?"

"Let me save your night. You came all the way in here, and it's a shame for you to go home without enjoying yourself."

"Oh really? And how do you intend to save my night?" she scoffs, eyes glinting. She's playing with me, I can tell.

"I'd rather show than tell, but… if you insist." I run my thumb along the bluish veins at her wrist, her pulse fluttering beneath my touch. "I'd begin by taking you to my private room, so we won't be disturbed. I'll ask you about your hard and soft limits, your likes and dislikes, before I'll ever consider easing you out of that little slip of a dress." I trail my eyes down the length of her body to the shoes that caught my attention earlier. "And I'd insist you leave those fucking shoes on. They're ridiculously hot."

Her breath catches, and I smirk at her dazed expression.

She clears her throat, shaking off the feeling. "Is that so?" She tries to hide how my words affect her. She's hooked.

I nod. "And that earring of yours." I run my free hand up to her ear, touching the delicate metal as I tuck her hair behind her ear again. "It makes me think you wouldn't mind if I tied you up… just a little."

"Fucking hell," she breathes, her clutch clattering to the tabletop from her limp fingers. I hold out my hand, waiting for her to slide her smaller one into mine. "Fine." Our fingers interlace, and my heart nearly skips a beat as she allows the touch.

We walk through the curtain toward my private playroom, and I can't help but notice how she carries herself. Confidence has her chin lifted, walking beside me like an equal and not behind me—unlike my usual girls, who have their heads down like a sub without the conversation. It doesn't bother me, and if anything, it makes her even more appealing.

I hold the door open and motion for her to go in first. "After you."

My duchess steps in, turning slowly to take in the large four-poster bed, the black sheets, and the sleek lines on the furniture. Her expression gives away nothing. "So… this is where you bring all the new girls?"

"I don't typically play with the new girls, no." The door closes with a soft thud and a click as I turn the lock. My steps, muffled by the silky nap of the rug, disguise my approach. I lean in close, the tantalizing smell of her perfume drawing me in. "Tell me your limits, Duchess."

"No choking, and, uh, keep it soft. Also, um, green-yellow-red for check-in?"

"Good girl," I praise. "Anything else? Blindfolds, restraints?"

"Those are good." The words escape her on a single breath, sounding more like a single word.

"You're full of all kinds of secrets, aren't you?" I slide my hands along her arms, smiling at the gooseflesh that pops up in my wake.

"Sometimes a girl just knows what she wants."

Cheeky, I think, pulling my tie loose from my neck. "I'm going to blindfold you with my tie. No peeking."

"Yes, Sir."

Perfect. She's so fucking perfect for me. Looping the material over her eyes, I fasten it with a simple knot and let the tails loose to dance in her long hair. Leaning into her neck, I allow myself a soft inhale of her perfume before purring in her ear, "Comfortable, Duchess?"

"Perfectly," she whispers.

My hand tightens slightly on her loose hair, tilting her face up to mine, even though she can't see. A soft gasp of surprise escapes her lips, her cheeks flushing. "Come again? I think you forgot something."

"I'm comfortable. Thank you, Sir."

"So responsive," I murmur, letting her hair fall across my fingers again. "May I twist your hair in a braid? I have an extra band."

"Please and thank you, Sir."

I make quick work of sectioning her silky hair between my thick fingers, reveling in the smoothness before throwing it in a quick braid. I drop a kiss against the back of her neck, pleased with her presentation.

"So fucking beautiful," I murmur, dropping another kiss on her exposed neck. I trace my fingers along the strap of her dress, the silky fabric glimmering in the dim light, and close around the pull of the zipper, giving it a slight tug. "Give me a color, Duchess."

"Green, Sir."

"Good girl," I praise, dragging the zipper down slowly, allowing the fabric to drift away from her soft skin. I slide my fingers along her exposed back, goosebumps rising in its wake. I walk around in front of her, hands on her waist, and kneel, gritting my teeth as I feel a twinge in my hip. Fuck being an older hockey player. Giving a soft tug, her dress slips off her shoulders, the top pooling at my hands. Gathering the fabric, I slide it down.

"Put your hands on my shoulders, Duchess. Step out of the dress." Dutifully, she steps up, first with one heel, then the other, allowing me to pull the dress away from her ankles. "That's my girl."

"This would be easier if I could see where I'm going," she starts, adding hastily, "Sir."

"Almost done," I murmur, rising to my feet and draping her dress across a nearby chair. "Come this way and kneel."

Guiding her carefully to the enormous bed, I help her to a kneeling position in the center of the dark duvet. Her hands rest lightly on her thighs, palms up, with no instruction. She can't see me, but I can't stop smiling with pride. Usually the first time with someone new is clumsy, the moves familiar but not instinctual, but she behaves for me like we've done this together a million times. I pause, wondering if maybe we have and I just didn't remember her, but no. I would have remembered her, I'm sure of it.

I enjoy the view of her as I take off my own clothes, laying them across the chair. I breathe allowing the calm comfort to settle over me. The order, the rules, they give me peace. Her head tilts in my direction as my belt buckle jingles, trying to track where I am and what I'm doing.

"Curious about what the plan is, Duchess?"

"Maybe a little."

"Second guessing the blindfold? Give me a color."

"Yel—green. Sir."

"Tell me what you need. I want you to be comfortable."

"Don't leave me in silence. It makes me nervous. I won't know if you've left me alone like this. Touch me or tell me, please."

"Let me fix that." I drop a knee beside her on the bed, resting a hand on her thigh, sliding my fingertips north along her smooth skin. "I enjoy doing both with you. A man could get addicted to touching you like this."

"Thank you, Sir," she whispers, a gasp dropping from her lips as I swipe a finger along the seam of her thighs.

"Spread." She complies with such ease, allowing my hand room to move as I slide the other up and down her spine, guiding her down onto all fours, and then to rest on her elbows. "Good girl."

She shifts under my touch, seeking more pressure from my fingers, and I clap my hand across her ass, the crack of skin on skin echoing. She gasps in surprise, but the clench of her muscles tells me it wasn't an unpleasant surprise. My duchess enjoys a little light spanking. Noted, I think with a grin.

"Please, Sir, please," she moans when I slide a finger inside her to my knuckle.

"Lean forward, put that pretty ass in the air for me." Again, she drops forward onto her elbows, posing just as I asked. Perfection. I need to get her real name before she leaves so we can set up a proper date. I know I won't be satisfied with just this one time. "You should see how gorgeous you are, laid out like this for me."

"I know what I look like," she chirps, swaying her hips back and forth for me.

I drop another slap onto her perfect ass, enjoying the pink outline of my hand on her skin.

"Don't get smart now," I warn. "Color."

"Green, Sir," she responds quickly, sighing as I slide my palm over the spot I just hit, soothing the burn.

"Good girl."

Every touch draws a new sound from her until she's literally begging, "Please, I need you, please." Her babbling pleas are music and I can't deny either of us this. Playing with her has to be my new favorite thing ever.

Sliding behind her, I sheath myself in the condom, teasing her gently with the tip. "Tell me again."

"Green, Sir, we're so, so green. Please." She's as eager for this as I am.

I press forward, eyes rolling back as she squeezes me. "So fucking tight," I growl, feeling her walls flutter around me. We've done virtually nothing, and I'm already on the verge of coming. It's never like this. Ever. "Look at you, taking me so well."

Her gasps and whimpers drive me to thrust harder, and my balls tighten. *Shit, I'm not going to last.* Tugging her hips back to mine, I sit back on my heels, pulling her upright to straddle my thighs. As I wrap my arms around her, my left hand grasps at one of her full breasts while my other hand dives lower for her clit. She mewls, rocking against me.

"That's it, take what you want, Duchess," I whisper, dropping my lips to her neck. The way I want to kiss her senseless, when I never want to kiss anyone, is unbearable. It's too intimate for this playtime.

Fuck it.

Against my better judgement, I grasp her chin, pulling her head back so I can reach her lips. She still tastes like cranberries and citrus, and I never want this to end. She pants against my lips, and I groan as she tightens around me. I'm never going to last like this

"Come for me, Duchess," I command, gritting my teeth to stave off my own. I at least need to feel her come first before I do. Fireworks erupt behind my eyelids as I let go, euphoria overtaking me as I follow her over the edge. Holy shit. The edges of my vision darken, and I hold on to her, whispering praise in her ear as our breathing slows.

"Oh my God," she mutters, slowly leaning forward out of

my embrace, the movement letting my softening dick slide free.

"Yeah, that." I frown a little, realizing we're done. "Um, just so you know, I'm not usually that fast."

"No?" she retorts with a laugh. "Don't get me wrong, that was quicker than I expected, but I'm not mad about it." With a sigh, she reaches to remove the blindfold. "This may be the hottest think I've experienced, ever."

The silk slips off of her face, falling limply on the bed. She freezes, her face morphing from sated and happy to absolute horror.

"Oh my God, you're— Shit, I gotta go," she gasps, shoving off my chest. Moving faster than the rookies at practice, she's off the bed, scrambling to pick up her scraps of clothes, and running for the door.

Like Cinderella, she has left me after the best night I can ever remember, and I don't even know her name.

OH. My. God.

My pulse pounds relentlessly in my ears as I stare sightlessly at my screen, thumbnails of smiling hockey players staring back at me. Two days ago, I did something reckless—I let Robicheaux talk me into going to this exclusive club in the North End, and rumors are that it has a secret members only sex club in the back. Of course, he didn't have the common decency to even show up, leaving me hanging by myself at the bar. Bored, I wandered around and I stumbled into the secret part, somehow, by myself. Then there was the ridiculous Chad guy, with his whole faux-Dom thing. So gross, I think with a shudder.

And then there was the guy with the wolf mask. Ridiculously hot, and just exuding that thing that powerful men do. Jesus, he made my knees weak as he came over. And the way he made the other guy leave, saving my night, it made him even hotter. I could have turned down his offer of a private room, but there was just something about him I felt drawn to, and that should have been my red flag. I should've known better. He was too smooth, and felt too familiar. That deep voice, even under the heavy bass of the music, had a tone I felt drawn to.

Of course he was familiar, I've listened to that tone daily for the last year in some format or another. Apparently last night I had my world rocked by one of the Ice Wolves, and I don't know who. So much for my "no touching the players" rule.

Taking off the blindfold and seeing that tattoo, I know I panicked. I've had that tattoo burned onto my retinas from social media posts. It's the same tattoo that graces the chests of several Ice Wolves players—enough of the roster to make me anxious. At last count, six current players had that same wolf head embedded in their skin after the last playoffs run. One of them was Elliot Moxley, so too blonde, and also dating my coworker. One was my best friend, Jean-Luc Robicheaux, and I'd know him anywhere; also, he would have never, we're far too close of friends for that. This leaves Valentin Bishop, our goalie, or the weird D-man, Mark Thompson. I shudder, thinking of Thompson. No, I don't think he can be cool enough to be attractive. He constantly tells me how to do my job. Bishop though, I could handle it being him, but what would he say if he knew it was me? Or maybe I'm blowing this all out of proportion and I made it up in my head. No, Bishop wouldn't be caught dead at someplace like that.

Groaning, I drop my head back onto my desk with a dull thud. What a freaking mess.

"J Lo!" Robicheaux's thick French-Canadian accent yells behind me, with the "J" softened to sound almost more like "shay."

Jumping with a screech, I grapple to stay upright in my chair. "Damnit, Robes!" I growl, righting myself with a huff. "Don't scare me like that!"

"Sorry," he chuckles as he settles a fresh coffee cup by my keyboard and hands off a small paper bag to me. The label on the cup shows my exact order with my name and a smiley face scrawled over it in teal marker. "Want one? I got an extra."

"Thank you." I take his offered chocolate croissant. I smile, enjoying the smell of the warm, buttery pastry, but frown when I remember why he's here. "But I'm still mad at you for the other night. Breakfast doesn't fix this."

"I said I was sorry," he whines with an obnoxious pout, batting his stupidly long lashes. It should be illegal for a man to have photo-ready lashes like that without help.

"You abandoned me at the club, and some idiot accosted me! Where were you?"

"I—" he starts, stopping his words with his lips between his teeth, gripping the back of his neck nervously with a sigh. "I fell asleep watching Hallmark movies," he murmurs, barely loud enough for me to hear.

My head tilts as I process his statement, or at least, I try to. The last words tumbled from him so quickly they felt like one giant word. "Say again?"

Sighing again, he ducks his head, cheeks pink with embarrassment. "I said I fell asleep watching Hallmark movies."

"You cannot be serious, Robes." A laugh bubbles out of me before I can stop it. "Hallmark movies? You stood me up for which one? The one with the big city exec getting stranded at the only inn in town, owned by the handsome single guy who has a faithful dog?"

"Yeah, I—" His face scrunches up like the words hurt. "They always have a happy ending! It's nice, okay?"

I press my lips together before I can slip another giggle at him. He's so serious when it comes to his movies, and I love that about my friend. I rest a hand on his forearm, smiling. "Sure, I get it. But, like I said, I was alone in a club and some dude harassed me."

A stony mask covers his face. "Who was it? What's his name? I… just want to talk." His giant arms cross over his thick chest as he straightens up to his full height. He looks ready for a fight.

Shrugging, I pick up my coffee. I appreciate his protective streak, it's what we've bonded over in the past. "I don't know. There was some kind of masked party theme going on. I'm glad they had masks at the door or I would've felt really out of place."

"Masked party? They don't— Oh…oh no, J Lo, you mean you went into the *club* club? The part behind the velvet rope?"

"That's what I said. I went to the club, and the guy had a mask on."

"You weren't supposed to go into that part of the club! That's…" He pauses, peeking around to see who was in earshot, whispering, "That's not a normal club."

"Well, where else was I supposed to wait for you while you dreamed of puppies and opening a bakery in a small town, you overgrown Golden Retriever?"

Roby sighs, running a hand through his dark, shaggy hair. "I'm sorry."

"It's okay, he got scared off by some manager guy, and he made sure I was safe." Not the full truth, but also not a full lie either. "It wasn't that bad of a night after that."

"Maybe we can try it again this weekend? We could go Friday night. I won't fall asleep this time. I promise."

"No way! I'm not going back in there again. I've seen plenty." I can't tell him I might have ran into another player there, or that I tripped and fell on his—

"Come on, J-Lo, I promise I'll make it worth your while."

"You have an away game this Saturday anyway, dork. Just…" I sigh, "we'll find some time to hang out later, okay?"

"Deal!" He shouts, fist pumping the air in a version of his post-goal celebration. "I gotta get down to PT, but I'll call you, k?"

"Yeah, okay, buddy. See ya, Robes!" I call out, waving in

his general direction as he leaves. "Looks like a cinnamon roll, is a cinnamon roll," I mutter to myself.

"Sounds like you had an exciting weekend," Ronni's voice carries over the partition between our workspaces. I grin, seeing my work bestie peeking over the partition. We started interning together and we've been inseparable ever since.

"I've had better." It's not a complete lie; standing in a room by myself is one of my worst fears, and for a minute, the interaction with the one guy felt off. But after that…

"We should do something this weekend. The team is out of town, and we haven't had a girls' night in ages. We don't even have to go out! Self-care at home, to recharge sounds amazing."

I smile, nodding in agreement. "I'm totally down with a night of romcoms and face masks! Your place or mine?"

NEVER HAVE I ever obsessed over a woman like this. In all my years, I've never considered what happened in—or who stepped into—my club, especially days after the fact. But I can't get her out of my mind, no matter how hard I try.

A dozen crystal bottles of varying shapes and colors checker my desktop, scattering prismatic rainbows across the leather blotter. My Duchess—because yes, she is mine—had to have worn one of them the other night. This was the second delivery from my assistant, who I sent to scour the city for me, and so far, none of them match. My teeth grind, frustration bubbling inside me. My tie, the same one I blindfolded her with, hangs loosely from around my neck, her perfume still faintly clinging to the silk. How hard can it be to find one woman in a city this size? Rhetorical question, I know. I'm in a major metropolitan area that is only slightly smaller than the state capital, so it isn't going to be easy to find her.

The scent left clinging to my tie is fading, and I can't let that happen until I find her. Delicate, sweet, I'm addicted to it. But none of these bottles are her scent, and I need it in ways words cannot describe. If I can't find her, I need to find this.

Growling, I pick up my phone, pressing send on my assistant's number.

"Good morning, Val. What can I do for you?" Conway's smooth voice comes across my speaker as I picked up a delicate pink bottle.

"Hey, Con, these aren't it."

"What do you mean, they're not it?"

"The bottles. The scents are wrong." I sigh, setting one back down. "Take them back, please."

"You know this might be easier if I had something to go on," he counters, an argument we've had every morning since Sunday when I called him at sunrise to go shopping. "You said you had a sample—"

"And you're not taking it. I don't want it lost." Chicken, I think to myself, you don't want him to have it because you don't want him to know. Or, worse than that, lose it. "Just go look for more." I grimace at how needy I sound, then add, "Please."

I hear him sigh, then a car door closing. "Will do. You know some of these stores have a restocking fee."

"And you know I gave you unchecked access to my business accounts. It's fine."

"Roger that. I'll be over in about thirty to grab them, then."

"Let yourself in, you know the code. They're all in the office on my desk." With a frustrated sigh, I step into my shoes. "I'm heading to the arena."

We say our goodbyes, and I wrap the tail of my tie around my neck, tying a practiced knot at my throat. Maybe she'll come back to the club this weekend. Maybe I should look at the membership records to find out who she is. Or, maybe I'll forget all sense of propriety and try to dig through camera footage at the door to see her ID.

That didn't sound like any psycho stalker bullshit behavior at all. Nope. Totally reasonable behavior of a guy who just wants to meet the girl he can't stop thinking about again.

"God, Bishop. Enough of the romantic, sappy bullshit," I grumble into the empty room, shaking my head at my ridiculousness.

Either way, I need to walk into the arena with a clear head; I'll deal with all of this mess later.

———

I heave a sigh as I turn off my car, gather my phone from the console, and climb out of my car to make my way from the reserved parking to the locker room entry. Game day entrance is always a production, and I'm honestly not feeling it today, which isn't like me. I don't mind doing my part for the team, usually, but I'm distracted today with thoughts of dark hair, shiny piercings, and breathy moans.

I want to find this woman more than I want to play hockey. That never happens. I need to remind myself that nothing is more important than the game. Shifting my hand down my shirt, I smooth the wrinkles out on my tie, catching another faint wisp of her perfume again, before wiping my hands down my thighs.

As soon as I walk into the tunnel from the parking lot, I'm going to be on camera—Jessica and Ronni have built a following for game day fits and behind-the-scenes interactions. I appreciate Jess has a professional yet friendly relationship with us players. Where she could be very firm like Ronni, she tries to be engaging without crossing any lines that would get us in trouble with HR. I want to get to the locker room and settle for the day, I really need to just get this over with.

Fuck, I don't want to talk to anyone today. Especially hot brunettes…get your shit together, Bishop.

Sure enough, there they are. Ronni has a camera trained

on where I'm entering, and Jessica is just around the corner with a tiny mic talking to Roby and Kozy. For as long as anyone has known them, they have always lived, worked, played, and gone to school together. Inseparable. Rumor had it they "play" together too, but even if it's true, that's their prerogative. Who am I to yuck anyone's yum? Good for them, honestly. Sharing is caring.

Groaning inwardly, I flash a smirk toward the lens that I'm glad is capturing my best side. Anything for the fans, I remind myself. Ronni nods her head in approval, apparently pleased with what she sees on the screen, and as she smiles at me, I wink at her.

"Come on, Roby, let's go," Kozlov says, dragging Roby along with him toward the locker room door.

Jessica glances up at me, her dark hair hanging loose over a white Ice Wolves hoodie. I flash a smile, in case my interaction with her is also caught on camera. "Hey, Valentin, you got a second?" Her question comes out in a rush, slightly breathless, and dare I say, nervous? Why is she nervous about talking to me? She restlessly adjusts her hair around her ear, the black strands making a curtain around her face, as opposed to tucking it out of her face like normal.

"Anything for the 'gram, right?" I tease, flashing a smile toward the camera. She blushes, breaking eye contact with me, and I can't ignore this feeling in my chest. I love seeing her that way and wonder for a split-second just how far down that blush goes.

Not that I'd be against it, she's beautiful and intelligent, easy to talk to, but professional boundaries exist for a reason. Power imbalance in the hockey world is a real and pervasive thing, and the trend of turning us into eye candy is a double-edged sword. Her balance in building engagement without treating us like pieces of meat is refreshing. I appreciate the care she takes, and that it mirrors my own boundaries at the club. What happens there, stays there, and all of that. Except for last weekend…

God, stop it, you obsessive pervert.

"You got that right. So, the question I'm asking everyone today is what is the best post-game snack?"

I can't give the truthful answer. The best post-game snack is winding down at Caissa. Especially with someone that doesn't give me her name, runs away without aftercare, and invades my every waking moment for days.

"Something high in protein helps. Lots of water to rehydrate. Bananas are good too, they keep the cramps away."

"Wow, that's, um, yeah. Thanks, Bishop." My forehead crinkles. Why does she sound so weird?

"Post-game dehydration is a problem, and it helps. I've learned a few things over the years."

"Who–I mean, what's your favorite? Or, um…yeah, favorite? "

"Two questions on the way in? I'm flattered."

"You were vague, I'm asking for clarification," she answers flatly. "Anyway, everyone else had really specific things that I could clip and I'm not sure if I can snag anything…I'm rambling. Sorry. Anyway, just…anything specific?"

"Fair enough." I pause, thinking hard. "Honestly, some of Woody's peanut butter cookies work fine. There's protein powder in it, they're so good. But I'm not against going to Nico's for grilled chicken and vegetables, either."

"Thanks for your time, Bishop. I appreciate it. Good luck at the game tonight!"

"Anytime. It's been a pleasure, ladies," I respond, waving at them both before walking into the chaos of the locker room. That had to be the strangest pre-game I've ever had.

Setting my phone on the wooden shelf, I start my pre-game routine, trying to push the thoughts of how awkward her interaction with me was, and wondering why it bothered me so much that everything felt different after last weekend.

I SHOULDN'T BE HERE. I should be at home, binge-watching reality TV, and not at the club where I definitely had the best sex of my life with a team player, just to see if I can find him again to confirm my suspicions.

Best case scenario? Bishop. Worst case? A married player? I shudder to think. My mind is a swirling mess, the vodka cranberry I'm sipping just barely numbing the rough edges of my thoughts. On one hand, I want to know who he was so I can apologize for overstepping boundaries. On the other hand, I wonder if we can do it all again, and maybe keep it a secret. But do I really want to know who he is? Or do I want to keep the anonymity going? Could we have another night of fun? Please, I beg on the altars of all things holy, let it be Bishop and not Thompson. The only other one I can think of makes me cringe and I'll be so sad to find out it was the mansplaining idiot on Defense. I really, really hope it isn't Thompson.

Guilt gnaws at my gut; it feels like what we did that night could have crossed so many professional boundaries. But we both consented to it sexually, right? Can you consent to something without knowing all the pertinent details? And does he even remember me? If it is Bishop, like I suspect, he has a reputation of being a man-whore, so it could have very well just been another meaningless, faceless hookup for him and I'm just making a big deal out of nothing.

This was a mistake. I should leave.

With a sigh, I pick up my glass, and finish the last of the drink. As I prepare to stand, a familiar purr comes from behind me, "Hello, Duchess."

I freeze. "Hello," I respond, the words a raspy whisper. I clear my throat and try it again. "Hi."

"Hi? That's all I get?"

"Sorry. Hello, Sir?"

"That's my good girl, but that wasn't what I was looking for. You left so quickly I didn't get to properly take care of you afterward."

I bow my head, still refusing to turn and make eye contact with him. "I'm sorry. That was–"

"That was dangerous, Duchess. Something frightened you. If I did something you didn't like, if I took it too far and you were uncomfortable—"

I nod shakily, eyes locked on the glossy bar top in front of me. He still hasn't moved to take a seat beside me, standing directly behind me, out of sight. It's like he knows wordlessly that I'm in no shape to see him fully.

"Are you comfortable talking to me about what happened?"

"I… I should. But I'm afraid of what you'll say. Or what it means." I know my reply is cryptic, but I just cannot say it here, in the open. "I think we need to talk, but I'm not ready to see you yet." I sigh. "God, that sounded rude. I mean—"

"No need to explain. We don't know who the other person is, and that's a big step. I respect that, Duchess."

I release a breath, feeling the tension between my shoulders loosen. "So how do we fix this?"

"I have an idea." His warmth envelops my back, and my

eyes instinctively close, soaking in the feel of him. A large hand, one I recognize as his, slides beside me, placing a key on the counter by my hand limply holding my empty glass. "Wait 5 minutes, then go to this room. I'll be there. No lights, no pressure. We can just talk. You have my word."

I slide my hand over the key, my pinky brushing against his warm skin and sending tingles up my arm. Grasping tightly to the metal, I nod again in agreement.

"Use your words, Duchess."

"I'll be there. Sir."

"Good girl. I'll be waiting."

He moves away, cool air striking against my back sending a shiver down my spine. Five minutes. I can wait 5 minutes, go to this room, explain in as little detail as possible what happened and leave. No one will know, our secret will be safe, and perhaps I can go back to work without worrying about the repercussions of that night.

Simple, right? Right.

I glance at my phone screen again, watching the time pass before I can go to the room.

Three.

Okay. So I go in, apologize for running out on him before, explain that I think I might know his real identity, wanted to respect his privacy, and leave it at that. We don't need to open that Pandora's Box. I'm happy leaving our identity unknown, I need to make sure that we're both okay with it.

Yep.

That's it.

Two minutes.

But what if he isn't okay with that? What if he wants me to admit who I am? Or who he is? I know he's one of about seven players with that tattoo, and two with long hair, which is more than I even want to know. Do I want to know for sure who he is?

One minute.

I stand on shaky legs, smooth down my skirt and move toward the hallway I remember from last time. *Oh God, this is it.* The dim light of the hallway glints off the metal in my hand as I make my way to the door number on the tag. Before I can talk myself out of it, I insert the key, turn the knob, and slip into the darkness within. The thin light from the hallway exposes a few details. All I can make out is he's sitting in a chair, his back to the door, head bowed. Waiting.

I'm going to be alone in a room with a man I don't know, in the dark.

Why the hell am I not scared shitless?

Because he treated you with respect last time, you idiot.

I let the door slide closed behind me, sinking us both into pitch black.

"Hello, Duchess." His words startle me in the dead quiet of the dark room. "Come and sit when you're ready." A faint glow from his phone screen illuminates the padded chair in front of him, his knees just inside the halo of light. It faintly glints off his long hair, showcasing his head turned away from me. I still catch a glint of metal. *He left the mask on? For me?*

I breathe easier; he's respecting my request of anonymity and not trying to figure me out. But what are the odds he'd even know it was me? Stepping in front of the chair, I lower into the velvet cushion as he turns off the screen, dropping us both into the dark again.

"I feel like I should apologize," I start, anything to break the silence.

"Would you like to elaborate?"

"I'm sorry I ran off like I did, I was scared and I didn't know what else to do."

"Was it what we did together?"

My head shakes forcefully, and then I remember he can't see me. "No, it wasn't what we did." My words rush out. "It was great, and you were perfect."

"You saw something when you took the blindfold off, I presume."

"I– I recognized a tattoo."

"Ah," he responds, sighing. "And you think you know who I am now."

"One of them. You have to live under a rock not to know that tattoo. And I avoid even casual relationships with athletes."

"Fair enough." He breathes deeply, letting the silence settle around us again. "But you came back tonight."

"As I said, I wanted to apologize because it felt wrong to leave and not say why."

"You're right. We didn't exit the scene appropriately. It's dangerous, and I don't play that way. Aftercare is non-negotiable for me." There's rustling, and then I feel a gentle, hesitant caress of his fingertip on my knee. "Can I touch you?"

"Yes, Sir."

"Let me properly take care of you, Duchess."

That single finger dances along the hem of my skirt, turning into the light pressure of two. He slides them under the edge of my knees, and pulls my chair closer to him. A squeak escapes me as my knees press into his inner thighs, now close enough I can breathe in his intoxicating cologne and the cool mint of his toothpaste. I could reach out and feel him again if I wanted. Oh my god, how I want to, I think. My hand twitches nervously on my thigh, my pinky brushing against the soft wool of his pants. The darkness is heightening my remaining senses like last time, making me hyper-aware of everything.

"Tell me, Duchess, what are you afraid of? Do you think we know each other outside this room?"

"I– I... Yes."

"Are you afraid you can't separate the two? That you can't differentiate between business, and," he pauses a beat, his thumb dancing along my skirt again, "pleasure?"

My breath catches, and I swallow hard. He's reading me like a damn book, and as raw and exposed as I feel, it's also freeing – like someone finally sees me. "I think it would ruin everything. Once the truth comes out there's no separating it."

"That's true, but maybe it wouldn't be such a bad thing."

I reflect on arena interactions with the players. All of them are cool, clinical, and professional. There's a boundary that we don't cross between admin and players, and what would it feel like if I put a name to this person? The more he talks, the more he sounds like…fuck, it is Bishop. I'm sure of it now. And there's no way in hell he will want to continue talking if he knows that it's me sitting here.

"This was a mistake." I start to rise from the chair on shaky legs. "Once we know who the other is, it could make things very awkward for the next several years."

"That's oddly specific, Duchess."

"I mean… all of your contracts are common knowledge. That's all." My damp hands smooth down my skirt. "I just wanted you to know I didn't hunt for you the other night, and that I hope even if you have an inkling of who I am, you won't mention this, outside of this room." I wave a hand aimlessly in the darkness, and start to move away.

I jump as his large hands wrap around my wrists, the slight callouses on his fingers sending goosebumps up my arms. "Duchess, what we've done was fully consensual, at least on my part. You were also enthusiastically consenting until we were done. Is that what you're worried about? The anonymity of the other night does not withdraw my consent. I still would have loved every moment of our encounter— with or without your name." A grunt escapes him. "Sorry, that makes it sound like it doesn't matter who was there; any hole is the goal, and that's not it. I just mean that knowing or not knowing who you are outside these walls, it was an amazing time, and I'd be open to doing it again, if you wanted. Our chemistry was off the charts."

"You're not wrong there," I whisper, releasing a shaky laugh.

"What if I said we could keep it just like this? No names, no identities. Would you stay here with me?"

"But you're..." I trail off as his hand skims up my forearm then back to my wrist again, the touch sending electric sparks to my belly, and my thighs clench.

"I don't know who you are, and you only think you know who I am. Remember? Even if you tell me who you are, I won't treat you differently."

"You swear? If this gets weird, I'll have to find a whole new tea— um, city." I clear my throat. "I wouldn't be able to stay here knowing we can run into each other again," I fib.

My pulse jumps under his fingers caressing my wrist, and I cringe. I just about gave up where I knew him from. Did he notice? Oh, God, don't let him notice, do *not* let him notice...

"I swear. I just want to know when I can see you again. Are you free Friday?"

"Not—" My words stick, and I clear my throat a little. "Not tonight?"

"No, Duchess, you're not in the right headspace to play. You've been all stressed out about this. I can feel it."

"Oh, I thought..."

"You thought I would forget what I said about not touching you unless you wanted me to? I didn't forget."

"But what if I... never mind." I take a step away. He pulls on my hand gently, throwing me just off-balance enough I land across his thighs. Oh, I forgot how big those thighs were.

"Say the words, Duchess. I'm not fucking you tonight, but if you need me to take the edge off..."

"Please," I whimper, barely moving the air between us before his lips land on mine, and I melt under his touch in the dark.

"Please what, Duchess? Tell me what you need." His touch scorches my inner thighs as he slips his hand under my dress. "Or better yet, show me." My knees slide farther apart, granting him the space he needs, and he groans in approval. I let my head fall against his shoulder, humming an affirmation. His blunt fingers wander along the edge of the lace, light touches that send electric sparks through me.

"You've been like this all night?"

I don't trust myself with words. "Maybe," I whisper, a soft sound of surprise escaping me as he presses into the fabric again.

"So wet for me" he murmurs against my ear, his breath sending shivers down my spine. "You've thought about this since you left, haven't you. Missing this, craving this." His fingers pull aside the lace, a thick finger just touching, a tease of what I want.

"Oh my God," I gasp, as he presses in, my eyes rolling back in my head.

"Look at you, you're a mess right now, grinding on my hand. Needy fucking thing."

My heart is pounding against my chest, and I can't stop the roll of my hips, pressing his hand between us. The friction is delicious and I can hear his breath catch. I do it again, feeling him harden against me.

"I need–I...please." Again, I press restlessly, trying to get more contact.

"Use your words, Duchess," he growls against my neck, pressing a hot open mouthed kiss against my jugular. "I want to hear it from you."

I can't think straight with this sensory overload, each touch from him amplified. Never have I ever gone from zero to the verge of exploding, especially without either explicit instruction or doing the work myself. With him, it's like everything is exciting, new, but also familiar at the same time. He pulls away slightly, only to replace his one finger with two, his thumb laser focused on my clit in dizzying circles.

"Oh shit," I gasp, and with one last press, I detonate. Stars explode at the edges of my vision as my orgasm crashes over me. I sob out my release in the crook of his neck, his woodsy cologne soothing me.

"Good girl," he praises, slowing his touches and with-drawing, carefully righting my clothing as I rest bonelessly against him, breathing heavily. "Do you feel better now?" Words are too hard, so I just rock my forehead against him, humming an affirmative purr. "That's what I like to hear." A large hand smooths up and down my side, the soothing action hypnotic as I settle against him. "Are you falling asleep on me now?"

"No, just comfortable." I sigh happily, my own arms wrapping around his large torso. "But I should probably get up and leave."

"Will I see you Friday?" His question reminds me of where our conversation had started.

"I think so," I respond. "But how will I know it's you?"

"Keep the key. Be here at 7:30. I'll watch for you."

Carefully, I stand off his lap on shaky legs, his hands a firm balance against my hips. I hear him get up as I step away, a guiding hand staying on my back as I step in the dark toward the door..

"So, see you Friday," I say, sliding my hands up to find his broad shoulders, and then guide my lips to his.

"Until Friday, Duchess."

The door opens slightly, the dim light from the hallway almost harsh in the pitch darkness of the room. Without peek-ing, I walk out the door, and smile as I hear the latch click behind me. He didn't peek either.

I can't help but grin as I think ahead. I have a date this Friday with my mystery man.

THE DOOR CLICKS SHUT behind her, and I lose all semblance of control.

My shaking hands fly to my belt, the buckle taking far more effort than necessary to unclasp. I tear at my restrictive clothing, coordination failing me as I fight the zipper, the process taking far longer than it ever has in my life. I've never been this so worked up. I can still feel her on my fingers, and if I can just get…

I curse between gritted teeth as I wrap my hand–still damp with her release–around my aching cock, the damp/dry slide of my palm a new example of torture, and I revel in the feeling. This isn't going to take me long. I fall forward, my forehead resting on my forearm against the cool wood, and give myself a few punishing strokes, feeling my balls tighten in response. I need to come so hard, so fast, right fucking now. My eyes roll back in my head as my orgasm slams into me, painting the door with my release.

"Holy shit," I gasp, trying desperately to catch my breath as I come down, little stars forming at the edges of my vision. I blindly tap along the wall in the dark, trying to turn the dimmer switch on.

I don't even know who she is, but she's going to be the death of me.

———

This meeting could have been an email.

I lock my "autograph smile" on my face and listen as the same three people regurgitate the same information in different ways. Again. Internally, I'm screaming in frustration because these are precious hours of my life and career that I will never get back. Note to self: listen to Conway when he says to let him field the video meetings on this shit for me.

My hips and back are screaming at me for sitting in these tiny ergonomic chairs instead of the regularly scheduled deep tissue massage and acupuncture that I should have been doing now. Regrets, I have a few. But whatever. I don't have that much time left as a team player, even if it's not enjoyable, I need to be present in the moment before it's gone. Who the fuck am I kidding? This still sucks. Make up your mind, Bishop, do you hate it or tolerate it?

"Sorry I'm late, gentlemen. Jerry had some last-minute additions to our team's presentation for you." I groan internally. I'm going to be here until I retire. I just want out of here, and then she comes in with presentation material? Fuck my life, this will be death by Powerpoint and I have no one to blame for it but myself.

"That's fine, Jessica, I'm sure it was worth the wait," Roger Andrews boomed from the head of the table.

I'm sure it's a dick move not even to look up when someone enters the room, but I can't be bothered to turn and watch her walk in. Even if I could listen to her read me the riot act and thank her afterward. Who am I kidding? She's easy on the eyes, and I enjoy working with her. Would I date her if I were serious about dating? Maybe. She could be a solid candidate but we work together, so that's an instant no.

Just because Moxley and Ronni did it, doesn't meant mean it will work out for me.

Blah blah quill, blah blah company ink. Or something.

"I think you're going to like it, sir." My dick twitches at the word, I smother a grunt with a cough. "Ronni had– Oh. Bishop, I didn't know you were joining us."

"Face of the team," I quip with a grin, looking up to find her surprised expression. What, like she didn't know I'd be here?

"We think you're really going to like these new promo plans, and the potential for increased revenue that we're projecting," she continues, her smooth voice sending a thrill down my back. *Settle down, Bishop.* "We have a partnership planned out with the Rockville Animal Shelter for a 'Pucks and Paws' event, with some great photo ops and VIP exclusives to auction off..." She trails off, opening a lap top and running a cable from her seat at the middle of the table toward the plug near me. I could reach out and finish plugging it in for her. It would be the gentlemanly thing to do, but why should I speed up the torture?

"The collaboration events that you and Ronni put together in the past have been great for ticket revenue," Roger replies, everyone's eyes on her as she fusses with the equipment again.

"Thanks, Roger, we're hoping the partnership is one that we can keep long-term— Oh, excuse me, Bishop, can I get in here?"

I glance up at her, the tenseness in her shoulders visible. Is she nervous? No way. Her heel wobbles under her as she shuffle-steps awkwardly, trying to get closer to the table between me and the neighboring board member. Shifting back in my seat, she reaches across the table in front of me to plug in her cable. And that's when I notice it.

The perfume. The same one lingering on my tie. It's fresh and bright and...no, it can't be her.

My heart races, excitement coiling in my gut like never before. That's it, that's what I've been trying to find! I glance over, subtly looking at Jessica in a new light. Could she be... No. She can't. She's too straight-laced for my club. It's just a coincidence. More than one woman can wear a scent. When the meeting is over, I'll just casually ask what it is that she's wearing, because I want to get a bottle for a friend. Casual, just a question. Then I can know what my mystery girl wears and stop hunting.

She's not wearing her usual team gear, or business casual. Today she's in a black dress with a jacket overtop, very "men's suit" styled, her dark hair in a twist, but in a hot secretary kind of way. And the shoes? I nearly choke on my next breath.

She's wearing the same fucking shoes from the other night. Jesus Christ.

It is *her*. There is absolutely no way that Jess from PR just randomly happens to wear the same perfume and the same shoes as my duchess.

Jess is Duchess. Holy shit.

Physically, I'm here, watching her set up her laptop for a presentation from hell, half-chubbed up in a room full of people. Mentally, I'm rehashing our time together in a whole new light. Prim and proper Jessica from the marketing team was in my club, telling me soft and hard limits. Calling me Sir. Riding my hand. Begging me for more. Clenching around my–

I can't focus on a damn word that they're saying right now because all I can see is her bent over the bed in my room at the club with those damned shoes. All the blood in my body is pooling in my lap, and my head feels fuzzy as the feelings overwhelm me. I try to pull in a calming breath and get a fresh hit of her perfume which just makes everything worse. The combination of the scent and my flashbacks makes my dick twitch against my zipper and I grit my teeth. *Don't come in your pants during a business meeting.*

I can make it through the next however long, talking with these men, letting Roger Andrews trot me around like a show pony, and without letting anyone know that I am suddenly, ridiculously turned on by the woman who is trying to share insanely boring details about dogs and players. Focus on that. Dogs, your teammates, work. Think of Robicheaux with a puppy. There you go.

Stay cool, Bishop. Don't get yourself dragged to Human Resources. Stay —

"Bishop? What are your thoughts?" Her voice drags me back to the present, and I stare at her through the fringe that came loose from my hair tie.

"I'd like to brainstorm with you after the meeting. Stay after with me."

She shoots me a look from down the table, eyes wide. I could almost hear her bratty retort about saying "please," or "well, that's rather presumptuous of you." I lift an eyebrow at her, encouraging her to proceed. I'd love to see how the team execs react to our back and forth if that comes out.

"That can be arranged, I have a couple hours before my next appointment if you have things you would like to discuss."

Nodding my head, I gnaw on my bottom lip to keep from grinning—or telling everyone to get the fuck out. Finally, I can't take it anymore. Knowing how Roger feels about showing off the team, I plot an escape. "Hey Roger, you know the rookies are getting extra ice time now. Have you shown them to your team yet?"

"I haven't, Val. Thanks for reminding me! How about we cut this short and go down to the rink?" I grin hospitably, watching the men from around the table gather their belongings, stand, and wander toward the door behind him. I sink back in the leather chair, watching them go. "Are you coming with us?"

"No, sir, I think Jess and I will stay and chat, like planned, if that's fine with you." Look at me. Amenable, professional. Team Player of the Year potential.

"You two have fun. No one scheduled time here for the rest of the afternoon, so take your time! I have high hopes for you two and this event."

"Thank you, sir, I appreciate it," I say, getting up to shake his hand. What I really want is to shove them all out the door. What I do instead is smile broadly and shake everyone's hand as they exit. Roger ushers the rest of his exec team out, then the room is ours.

And she has nowhere to go. She's all mine now.

I watch through the doorway as they all walk away, chatting between themselves as they wander to the elevator bank, and then slowly shut the door, turning the lock with the barest amount of noise. Jess is still typing away furiously on her laptop, the soft click of her nails the only sound in the room. Perfect.

I step quietly behind her, watching as she keeps typing, her focus on the email in front of her. Leaning close, I brush my nose against the shell of her ear, my eyes rolling back in my head involuntarily as I take in just another hit of her perfume on her neck.

"Hello, Duchess."

I. AM. In. Such. Big. Shit.

His heat against my back soaks through the silk of my dress, making me feel like we are skin-to-skin. Again. A shiver trickles down my spine, butterflies set loose in my gut at the memory of the last time we had been this close.

Valentin Bishop. Val to close friends and family. Bishop to his teammates. Goalie for the Rockville Ice Wolves. Not just any player, but one of the biggest veteran players on the team. And Sir, apparently.

"Excuse me?" The question escapes me on a soft exhale, not at all the strong, confident persona I try to exude at work. How did he break down my walls like this?

"You heard me. And I'm sure you know the last time you heard me call you that name, too."

"I don't know what you mean—"

"Don't lie to me, Duchess." His large hands press into the dark wood near my forearms, caging me in, leaving me surrounded by his presence. I couldn't go anywhere if I wanted to. I can feel him rubbing against my neck again, drawing another deep inhale. "What are you wearing?"

"Um, a dress? Calvin Klein, maybe?"

"Not clothes, even though I love this look on you. Your perfume. What are you wearing?"

"Oh," I sigh as he runs his nose along my neck again. "It's just some oils I threw together."

"Fucking amazing," he growls, breathing deep again.

"Bishop? What..." I trail off, words escaping me as Valentin freaking Bishop drops an open-mouthed kiss against my throat, his tongue pressing against my jugular. Jesus, I think as my brain short-circuits. "Shit! The door..."

"I locked it. No one is getting in here unless we want it." His words rumble against my skin, and I shiver. "I don't think I want to share you right now."

"We can't..."

"We can't do what?"

"We can't, we shouldn't do this."

"We can do whatever we want." Bracketing my jaw with his large hand, he tilts my line of sight to the fluorescent lights over our head. "What are they gonna do, Duchess? Fire us?"

"You? No, you're the main goalie and worth millions. The face of the team. Me? I'm a dime a dozen and totally replaceable. A hundred people want my job. I will definitely get fired."

"Absolutely fucking not. You're better than that, and I won't have you saying otherwise. You are perfect and priceless... and mine."

"No, I'm not. I'm just a girl you work with."

With a speed I didn't know he possessed, he stands upright, turning my chair around and pinning me with a glare. His hands lock around on the armrests, leaving me no choice but to rest my sweaty hands against my thighs and look up into that stern face, his green eyes piercing.

"We're going to talk about that low opinion of yourself later. For now, though? I want to talk about why you ran away from me Saturday night."

"I think you know why, Val."

"Don't call me that."

"Bishop, you know—"

"Don't call me that, either."

Sighing, I glance back up at him. "You really expect me to call you Sir here? At work?"

"No, that's unrealistic," he scoffs. "But you called me Valentin before."

"Why stop at Valentin? Why not Mr. Bishop?"

"Mr. Bishop is my sperm donor, and he's dead. Let's leave him out of this." His strong, stoic face scrunches up like he smelled something off. "You're the only one who calls me Valentin, and I like it."

"You're serious," I whisper in awe, twisting around to make eye contact as best as I can within the space of his arms.

"Always."

"God, I can't concentrate with you this close," I mutter, twisting the chair back around and leaning closer to the tabletop.

"You concentrated just fine before," he murmurs in my ear. "But I have a question for you."

"What's that?"

"Why did you run away from me?"

"What—what do you mean?"

"Why did you leave the club, Duchess?" His nose slides along my neck again, his giant hands holding my wrists against the armrests, scorching my skin with his own. A moan escapes me before I have the chance to think about it, and I curse to myself when I hear his dark chuckle behind me. "Did you think I wouldn't chase you?"

"I didn't think you'd figure out who I am. Or if you did, you wouldn't want—*this*—again."

"Oh, Duchess," he purrs behind me. "You have no idea what you do to me."

"It's not a good idea to fraternize," I argue.

"Do you really think that's going to stop us? I don't know about you, but that night was phenomenal. I haven't stopped thinking about it."

"Didn't you use that line to get me to go with you in the first place? You said that Chad guy would give me mediocre sex and that I'd be the best he'd ever had. What makes you different from him?"

"Cheeky. I like it." His nose passes along my pulse point again, drawing goosebumps in its wake. "But I think we both know you're wet, remembering how hard I made you come."

"Fine, it was good," I grumble. "But it doesn't mean we should do it again. HR will have a field day, and they won't fire their top goalie."

"They won't fire you either."

"Like you have any say in the matter? You aren't the head of HR, and we have a policy manual that says we never should've done anything in the first place."

"It's not stopping Mox and Ronni."

His point is valid; I can't deny it. And I hate that he's right. It was amazing, and I haven't thought of anything else since. "Maybe when you're not on the active roster?"

His deep chuckle sends a shiver down my spine. How can he do this without even touching me? "I don't think either of us wants to wait that long."

"It's not a matter of what we want, it's what keeps us out of trouble. I love my job, so I can't mess this up, no matter how good it was between us. Let me go." With a sigh I shift sideways in the chair, extract myself from his hold, and walk out of the room without another word. I can't think with him so close, and being here with him is far too tempting for either of us.

CHAPTER 7
BISHOP

THEY SAY the best way to get over someone is to get under someone else. I have my doubts about whether this is going to work. I can still smell her on my favorite tie, and it just gets me fired back up about her again.

I feel like a complete idiot, sitting at this table for two by myself, waiting for my date. She's already late. The waiter has already stopped by twice to check on me. I'm about to go ahead and just order dinner, then call it a night. If I have to be here, I at least want to get my protein in for the night, so I glance to see what I feel like. Something besides my usual chicken and steamed vegetables, because nothing about my week has been normal. I point at my empty glass, signaling to the bartender to bring me a fresh whiskey on the rocks, before glancing at my watch. One more drink, and then I'll decide on dinner.

Fifteen minutes late. A disappointed sigh blows free as I glance down at my phone screen, devoid of notifications. Not even a "trying to find parking" text. What a waste of my goddamn time.

If only I could get Jess here. She made herself clear, but I know she also won't leave me hanging for fifteen fucking minutes after our agreed time. She'd have been here early, reservation confirmed in the morning, and would have called ahead to move us into the back corner where she knows I like to sit best. Frustration bubbles up in me as I watch the clock ease closer to twenty minutes late.

"For fuck's sake," I grumble, throwing back my top shelf whiskey like water. It's official. I, Valentin Goddamn Bishop, have been stood up.

On autopilot, I dial Robicheaux. Maybe that dickhead will be available. Not that hanging out in my damn club was a step up from being home alone, but at least I'd have company there.

"Bish! What's up?" Roby's French-Canadian accent beams through the line, and somewhere in the back I'm sure I heard a gruff, "Why the fuck is he calling?" from Kozlov. The Russian isn't big on socialization—why those two are best friends, I'll never know. Polar opposites, those two. I think my sister, Viv, called them "golden retriever and black cat," whatever that means.

I may as well extend the invite to Kozlov too. "Hey, what are you two up to tonight?"

"We thought about heading to The Sin Bin. We haven't seen Joey in a bit and it might be good to go in. Want to meet us there?"

Going to somewhere that I don't own? Sounds like a solid plan to me. "Cool, I'll meet you there in a few."

Settling up my tab, I head for the door. Hanging out with coworkers isn't the worst idea for the night.

The Sin Bin is a cozy sports bar that my ex-teammate opened last year after shattering his knee. It's comfortable, casual, and not at all like mine. Where Caissa is dim lighting and throbbing beats on the dance floor, Ronan Josephs set up The Sin

Bin to be more of a sports bar hangout. Bright lights, no dance floor, no quiet corners. Still, it's a comfortable place to hang out with friends, and players can come without being harassed by fans.

I'm completely overdressed for The Sin Bin, but don't care at the moment. I strip my jacket off at the door, walking through to where Ronan is standing by Robicheaux and Kozlov, laughing at something Roby is saying. Approaching the three men I've built a solid off-ice friendship with, I nod at a few fans nearby who subtly wave as I pass. This is why we like The Sin Bin, it has good energy. We can relax here, and just be ourselves.

"RoJo," I call out as I get closer. Ronan turns to me, grasping my hand and pulling me in for a clap on the back.

"Val, long time no see," he returns. "Do you want your usual?"

"Please, thanks, man."

"Be right back," he tells us, before heading toward the bar and leaving me to slide into the booth beside Roby.

"Didn't expect to see you here so soon," Kozlov mentions in his typical serious tone.

"I was already out across town," I answer. "I was supposed to meet someone at Nico's and she didn't show."

"The great Valentin Bishop, stood up? Really?" Roby cracks. Koz and I both shoot him a dark look and he clears his throat. "Dude, that sucks, and I don't know why anyone would. You're amazing company. Anyway. Did you eat before you left?"

"Nah, I'll get something here. I'm due for a cheat day."

We pick up the menus and I allow my eyes to wander the bar, taking in the crowd. I'm happy that our friend has found some success after his career, and he seems happy. The tables are all full of fans, televisions mounted around the room show a variety of sports games. Fans wearing various sports gear talk animatedly amongst themselves in small groups.

And then my eyes land on my Duchess. I'd recognize that hair anywhere, and my jaw clenches tight as I take in her black dress and boots. She walks across the room to some boring looking dude in a sweater vest and khakis, smiling before shaking his hand.

Is she on a date? Who the hell shakes hands on a date?

"Is that…" I start before trailing off, remembering not only where I am, but who I'm with.

"Jess? Yeah, it looks like," Roby responds. "She said something about having a first date, but she didn't say it was tonight. Or here." I look at him sideways. "What? We're friends. She tells me things sometimes."

"He looks like a real winner," Kozlov snipes, his mouth turned into a smirk. "She's going to to hate this."

"Give them a chance," Roby chides. "It's just their first time meeting, and he looks nervous. She won't be into that, sure, but maybe he has other redeeming qualities. Besides, Koz, you have no room to talk. The first time we met, you wore an ugly Christmas sweater."

"It wasn't an ugly Christmas sweater, it was the team jacket they sent me."

"You two fight like an old married couple," I grumble, not looking away from the couple across the room. Roby and Koz stop bickering to look back over, too.

Jessica and her date continue talking, oblivious to the three large hockey players sitting across the room, staring at them. Her attention stays on the man talking to her, waving his hands animatedly, her smile relaxed and polite, hands folded in front of her. I've watched her take the same pose in the past at meetings. Her crossed ankles and tapping her foot impatiently. Bored. It's a pose that screams, "This was a meeting that could've been an email."

She's having a vanilla date and she absolutely hates it. I can't stop the laugh that escapes me.

Shit.

I try to hide my amusement behind my drink, but Kozlov's eyebrow lifts. He caught me.

"She hates him," I offer. "He might be totally into it, but she can't wait to leave. She has her professional pose on. You know, when she's trying to be polite because we're in public, but she really wants to smack us." There. I don't sound obsessed, just observant.

Robicheaux's nod seals it. "Yeah, she needs an out. We could invite her over—"

"Nope. I have a better idea. Be right back."

Before I can think better of it, I stand and walk over, staying in her blind spot. Her date is rambling on and on about something inconsequential about stocks and dividends. Hell, I'm bored *for* her. I pause behind her, back turned to them for a second as he continues. Finally hearing enough, I turn, resting my hands on the back of her chair, and lean close to her ear.

"Hello, Duchess."

THE WINE I sipped politely as Cody babbled about stock trends does nothing to dull my boredom. Jesus Christ, I can't wait for this date to be over.

"Hello, Duchess."

I feel my eyes go wide, my throat burning as I swallow wrong, choking on the last sip.

"Jesus... Bishop?" I wheeze, dabbing at my mouth with the paper napkin.

"Hey, Jessica. Who's your friend?" His words come out too casual, calm even, as I glance up to his face with an innocent smile, as if he didn't just give me the jump scare of my life. Words stick in my throat, so he takes matters into his own hands. Holding out his massive hand, he winks at me before introducing himself to my date. "Hi, I'm—"

"You're... you're Valentin Bishop," my date whispers, awestruck, as he slowly puts what I unfortunately know to be a cool, clammy hand in Bishop's.

Oh shit, I found a fan. A slightly slimy one with a weak-ass handshake, but still.

"The one and only. So, you're friends with our Jessica." His hand comes off the table to rest possessively on my shoulder. I know it's a dick move of his, marking territory that isn't really his, but I just…

Breathe. This nightmare has to end soon.

"Our Jessica? There's more of you?" I huff as I jerk forward away from his touch. What the hell is he doing?

"Yeah, Roby and Koz are over there." He motions at a table farther down the wall, where Robicheaux is grinning like a damned idiot and Kozlov stares in that emotionless way that is so hard to read. I should have known better, thinking that I could fly under the radar with them.

Oh my God, my first date from hell has been visited by the three biggest players on the team, and they've decided to go all "Big Brother" on me. I didn't even look for them when I came in.

"You work with these guys? How freaking cool is that?" Cody, or Cole—whatever his name is—screeches like a little girl.

"Yeah, I work with the Ice Wolves," I answer with far less enthusiasm than I usually give. I can already hear him begging for free tickets in the future.

"Yeah, she does all our social media, like the candid clips. She's a smart, sneaky thing." What should have been a compliment, coming from Bishop's mouth comes across with a tone that I can't quite place.

"Shoot me now," I grumble under my breath, picking up my clutch from the table. "Excuse me, I'm going to leave. Maybe we can try this again some other time. Somewhere else. On a night with an away game. It was great to meet you, Cody—"

"It's Cole…" I hear him trail off as he looks back up at Bishop.

I don't wait for a response. My pulse pounds in my skull as I storm off to the restroom. I have to get away; I need room away from the pressure of Bishop's presence.

The emptiness in the bathroom gives me a moment to

breathe, to find my center again. Wrapping my hands around the cool white tile on the counter, I let my head drop. Why is he here? Why did he insert himself while I'm on my date? Why can't he leave me alone?

The door creaks softly, allowing a soft draft before closing again. With a sigh, I start, "I'm sorry, I'll get—Bishop?"

His large form fills the doorway, arms crossed across his chest, his brows furrowed. "You looked panicked. I came to check on you."

That's it. I've had enough. Smacking my hands against the counter, I then turn to look at him. "You interrupted my date," I grumble. "I have a life away from the arena, you know."

"You do," he agrees, nodding his head once. "But I also know you were bored as fuck with plain mashed potatoes out there."

"Plain… what? Did you take a puck to the head again?"

"He had all the personality of plain mashed potatoes. No gravy. No seasoning. Just… bland. You were bored, and you were waiting to escape, anyway."

"That wasn't your call to make!"

"You don't deny that he had the personality of a bowl of dry instant mashed potatoes and you hated every minute of it so far, and you haven't even gotten through appetizers. You're welcome, you know, for the distraction." He shrugs, as if his chaos was inconsequential. "Besides, knowing what you were like at Caissa, he would have never kept up with you anyway. Pretty sure you would've eaten him alive before your first orgasm."

Hysterical laughter bubbled out of me. He can't be serious. "I can't deal with you, Bishop. The night at your club was a mistake."

"Was it really? It seemed like you really enjoyed it until the blindfold came off."

"That was before I knew it was you," I counter. "Separation of work and play."

"You say this like you're a government entity—separation of church and state. I don't know about you, but I know when to play and when to put it away. You want to tell me what to do all day at the arena? Cool. I'm game. I'll listen to anything you want. But I want you to do something for me, though."

"Oh yeah? What's that?" I'm going to regret asking, but it's not as if I could stop the words if I wanted to.

"Tell me it wasn't the most connected you've ever felt to anyone." He pushes off the wall, leaving the words hanging between us as he slowly stalks toward me. "Tell me it wasn't the best sex of your life and all you can think about. Tell me," he growls low in my ear, "that I'm not the only one obsessed with experiencing that electricity again."

"Val, I—"

"Tell me you don't want me to touch you again. Even now, when you think you're pissed at me, that your body isn't screaming for this."

My breath catches in my throat as I lift my head and make eye contact with him in the mirror. I recognize that determined gleam, the same one when he stands in the net, following the game play. His full attention on me, unwavering, makes my heart race.

"I can't— I can't say that."

I feel his satisfied hum against my back, as his hand slides across my hip. God, I shouldn't want this, but he's right—I do.

"I know you can't. Do you want to know why?"

"Why?"

"You were made for so much more than a quick fuck at a club, or that loser out there. You deserve more than that. Don't settle for vanilla to escape from me."

"No one can know about this. Any of this."

"I can keep a secret if you can."

"Nothing happens at the arena."

He grins, as if his victory is imminent. "I'll keep my hands to myself if you can do the same."

"Obviously I can, I'm the one setting the boundaries," I snipe.

"And no talk of the club. To anyone. You've never been there."

"Fine. I don't want anyone knowing about that either."

"It's like we're sharing a brain," he murmurs against my neck.

"I can't think when you do that." My head falls back against his shoulder and I feel him smile against my over-heated skin.

"Your sassy mouth is saying no, but your body is definitely telling me yes."

"I know," I sigh, sinking into the feeling of his arms wrapping around me.

"Come home with me."

I freeze. What are we doing? Shoving hard away from the counter, I step away from his embrace. "Like hell I will! What part of 'not sleeping with the team' did you not understand?"

"You're not sleeping with the team, Duchess. You're working out some pent-up stress. With me."

"Wow, how noble of you."

"I'm serious. I'm heading home now. Come over. I'll leave first, so it doesn't look like we're going together. Let me save your night, at least. You know I'm good for it."

"Oh, sure," I glare, crossing my arms across my chest. The motion draws his eyes down, , and I huff in frustration adjusting my uncomfortable stance again. "And you're totally not getting anything out of this."

"I am," he admits. "You're saving my night, too."

"What's to save? You're hanging out with your friends."

"What if I told you I'm only here with them because... I got stood up?"

An unladylike snort escapes me before I can stop it. "I'm sorry, what?"

"I had a date tonight. She didn't show up."

"I don't believe you."

With a sigh, he pulls out his phone, opens an app, and turns the screen to me. Sure enough, a text conversation confirming dinner earlier at Nico's.

"So you want me to come over because you're lonely and your Plan A fell through? You think I'm an easy back-up plan?"

"No," he snarls. "I want you to come over because I enjoy your company. I think you enjoyed mine as well. We're grownups and can separate business and pleasure. I've watched you do it before."

"And you know so much about my dating life... how? Also, I've never dated anyone on the team."

"Come on, Jessica. I've watched you at events and games. You can't tell the difference between your date and your coworkers."

"What the hell does that mean?" My arms cross in front of me, and I grit my teeth against screaming obscenities at him. *Swearing isn't dignified, I brought you up better than that*, I can hear my mom's voice say.

Keep composed. Stay calm. Hysterics are for the weak. Obscenities are crass and beneath you.

He grimaces, like he knows the wording is wrong. "I just mean that you know when to separate work time from play time. You can—and do—keep your professional boundaries firm. I agree, that's how it should be. And I truly think that we could, if given the opportunity, be able to have this arrangement off the clock without it bothering what happens on the clock. Is that better?"

He's not wrong, and I know it. Keeping my private life out of my professional life has always been important to me. Also, it has been hard to find that guy who can also keep the boundary in place. The last few charity events have been one-off dates because they couldn't listen when I said to keep their hands to themselves, and let me work still. To have someone who knows the rules and stands by them, enforced them—this may be something I can get behind.

"So what, outside the arena? We're friends with benefits?"

"Exactly. And at the arena or team events, we're just coworkers."

"What's the worst that could happen?" I mutter to myself.

"We just enjoy it until something permanent comes along."

"For either of us."

"Sure. For either of us."

"Fine. Deal," I say, throwing my hand out to shake on the deal. His eyes drop to my right hand, hanging between us, before scooping my fingers into his large hand, flipping the angle, and dropping a kiss against my knuckles instead. The same move he did in the club that set my skin on fire.

"Shit," I whisper involuntarily, as his breath tickles my skin.

"Go say goodbye to your vanilla date, Duchess. The car is outside already. I'll be waiting."

"Yes, Sir."

I CAN BE a gentleman and not maul her like a feral animal in the car. Or the lobby. Or the elevator. I repeat the mantra in my head as my brain races of all the things we can do tonight, my leg bouncing. There is no cool, calm, collected where she's concerned.

My gaze falls to Jess sitting as close to the window and away from me as possible. Her bottom lip is white where her teeth press into the flesh, and I bite back a groan as I think how badly I want my teeth to be doing that instead, tugging on it slightly. Would she gasp? Moan? Bite mine back?

Fuck, I'm gone for her.

The driver pulls up in front of my building and I fling the door open before the car even settles on its suspension, shooting to my feet and holding my hand out for her despite the protests of the driver.

I should've known my Duchess wouldn't comply, as she opens her own door on the opposite side to get out on her own. I shoot her a pointed look, my eyebrow arching as I look across the hood of the car as she steps up onto the sidewalk. Falling in step beside her, we walk into the lobby, the clack of her shoes echoing off the marble floors and then wait for the elevator in silence.

A soft smile is on her face, pleasant, like she's just being nice to the stranger standing beside her. Fine, I can play that game. I tug at my cuffs as the elevator gives a cheery ding before the doors slide open. I motion for her to enter first, then walk in myself, pressing the button for the penthouse. The doors whisper close, and then all hell breaks loose. My breath flies from my lips on an *oof* as the hellcat shoves me against the cool metal walls and pulls my head down to her level by my short braid.

"Fuck," I gasp before she latches her lips on mine.

On instinct, I reach down, palming her ass and lifting her before twisting to press her against the wall, putting myself in control of the situation again. Her heels lock at the small of my back, pulling me tight against her, and I groan into her mouth as my dick throbs with its own pulse between us. I feel lightheaded and drunk with her in my arms. And fighting for control? Usually, this would piss me off to no end, but with her, it may become my new favorite activity. Jockeying for the upper hand between us turns me on more than I can even think.

The elevator car slows to a stop, chiming to announce my floor. Without letting her down, I stride out into my hall with her lips pressed against my neck before latching onto my earlobe.

My knees nearly give out under her onslaught, and I curse as she giggles and does it again. Wrapping one arm around her back to hold her still, I punch in my door code blindly, groan in frustration as the light turns red, and stab the numbers again. Stumbling through the doorway and kicking it shut behind us.

Finally, she's right where I want her.

How she went from ice cold to hot on me, I don't know,

but I'm drowning in the onslaught. Her hands are everywhere, tugging on my tie, pulling on my hair, and twisting her nimble fingers in the strands.

"Keep this up and we won't make it to the bed."

"Then hurry up," she chirps back before fastening her lips over my jugular.

Jesus Christ.

I stumble up the stairs as fast as I can, dropping her lightly on the bed and getting to work on her zipper. Her hands fly to the buttons on my shirt, pulling the material away from me with a harsh yank. Feeling her bare skin against my own feels like sinking into a warm bath. I pull back with a groan, letting my gaze roam over her exposed flesh.

"Fucking missed this," I growled, shoving her dress past her waist, watching her nipples pebble in the cool air.

"Val, please," she begs, scraping her nails down my chest, grabbing at my belt.

"Try again," I grunt as she unfastens my pants, sliding her hand along my bulge.

"Please, Sir." This woman is going to kill me.

"I know. This is going to be fast." I grasp her wrists, pressing them against the pillows behind her, back arching and lifting her breasts to me.

I'm never one to rush, I like to take my time and enjoy the process, making the experience build. Tonight is not following the plan. I need her as much as I need my next breath.

"Go slow next time," she pants, answering my unvoiced thought. I'm glad to know we're on the same page.

"Good idea." I grasp the last scrap of lace on her, pulling it slowly down her legs before pressing her thighs together with my own, holding her down.

"Hurry up, you're going so slow," she whines, pulling her hands away from the pillow. I freeze, giving her a pointed look and waiting for her to settle back into the position I had her. "Please. I need you."

I slip my hand into my pocket, pulling out the condom I stashed there, and slide it over my length. Her eyes stay glued on my every move, hungrily watching me as I just touch my tip to her entrance.

Our groans hit at the same time as I slide home. Gritting my teeth against the urge to just slam into her like a feral animal, I pull back, relishing in the feel of her fluttering around me.

"Please let me touch you, please, please, please." The words pour from her lips so sweetly that I cave, pulling her arms from over her head where she instantly wraps them around my waist, grabbing my ass and pulling me deeper, closer.

"Greedy girl," I groan, grinding my pelvic bone against her. Swiping my thumb between us against her clit, she screams as she comes undone, her muscles clamping down tight on me.

I can't hold out. No amount of reciting statistics from hockey history will hold this back. My eyes roll back in my head as I come, thrusting into her, the world going fuzzy and dark around the edges.

"Oh my God," she whispers between panting breaths, as we both come down.

I get off the bed, standing on shaky legs to dispose of the condom, and then crawl into the bed beside her, pulling her into my chest and kissing her lightly. "There. Now we can focus," I whisper, running a hand down her back, just enjoying how her soft skin feels against me.

"Don't tell me the great Valentin Bishop, hardass of the Ice Wolves, is a cuddler," she says with a giggle, all while snuggling closer.

My palm lands on her ass with a sharp smack, making her

gasp and grind against me at the same time. "That was sassy. Behave, it's just a pause before we pick back up where we left off." I toy with one nipple, relishing in the feel of her.

Each touch keeps the fire stoked between us. As she rolls me onto my back, her thighs straddling my hips, all I can think is that tonight is going to be a very long, very enjoyable night.

———

The morning sun jars me awake. I never sleep this late. But holy shit I feel great. Refreshed. Maybe I need to have Jess over for a sleepover more often.

My Duchess.

I smirk, replaying the night before in my head and reach over, fully intending to wrap myself around her curves again.

And reach.

And reach farther, finding nothing more than a cool pillow.

She's gone.

I sit up, looking around for any sign that she's still here, maybe in the bathroom.

No. Every piece of evidence that she had been here is gone.

Like last night never happened.

Groaning, I throw sweatpants on and wander out of the bedroom to find her. She couldn't have gone too far without me knowing, right?

I stumble into my office, hoping maybe she wandered into another room, only to find everything almost exactly as I had it the night before.

Except for the smell of her perfume hanging in the air.

Tucked under the corner of the perfume bottle—her perfume—sits a folded over piece of paper. Picking it up with sleep-numb fingers, I look at the words scrawled on it in her loopy cursive.

Thanks for last night. — J

"Thanks for last night? That's it?" I mutter at myself in the empty room.

For the first time in forever, I actually feel… alone.

CHAPTER 10
JESS

I CAN STILL FEEL his touches on me, and it is driving me to distraction.

My cursor bounces on my screen, the document totally blank, and all I can do is stare into the whiteness and replay the events from the night before.

Who knew he had that in him?

I'm supposed to be putting together the posts for the latest call ups from our farm team to distribute to our social media, but all I can think about is how his hands felt on me, pressing me into his mattress, tugging back my hair while I—

Get a goddamn grip, Jessica.

I shake my head viciously, trying to clear away the racy images that I just cannot get out of my head. I can't think about him at work like this.

Does sending a booty call text the next day break the FWB code?

"Jesus, Jess, it's like you've never had mind-blowing sex before," I grumble to myself, shoving my keyboard away from me in disgust. *But it's true,* the little voice of dissent whispers to me, *and you've never had mind-blowing sex like that before.*

"What's that?" Ronni calls from behind the cubicle wall.

She has a whole office upstairs and she still insists she does her best work at her old desk here in the PR Pit, as we called it.

"Nothing, I'm just yelling at myself," I reply, standing. I snag my phone and coffee, preparing to leave. "I need some air, and I should go down to the ice for B-roll, want to come with?"

"I wish! I have potential donors coming in a few for an arena tour. I just came down here because it was closer. Have fun, don't let the boys give you a hard time!"

Cool. So I get to go see him without my Emotional Support Bestie. I can do this, it's not like this is the first time. I'm a big girl.

Stepping through the tunnel into the rink space, I let the sounds of practice relax me. I love being in this space, watching the players work together, finding the best shots to highlight for upcoming games. Robicheaux and Kozlov are running some kind of defensive drill together, skating toward Bishop in goal. His hair must be down, the dark strands hanging out beneath his mask on top of the stark white shoulders of the practice jersey. Behind the cage, his dark eyes are laser-focused on the duo, tracking their movements. He's in his element, where he belongs. I can't imagine this man anywhere else in his lifetime.

Where the hell did *that* come from?

"Focus," I hiss to myself, picking up my camera to take a short video of the trio. The views on that will be insane, and a great way to highlight the game this weekend.

"Hey, Jess, how ya been?" I pause the video as Elliot Moxley, reaching across the boards for a green water bottle.

"Not bad, and you? Feel ready for Saturday's game?"

"You know it! Are you going to tell me what the fit check questions are this time?"

"Never," I respond with a laugh. "You know the deal. No cheating. I don't care who your girlfriend is."

Behind him, a whistle blows, and I watch players start to approach, some waddling down the tunnel to the locker room. "Oh, it's tape time for A-team. Gotta jet! See you later!" With an awkward fist bump, Elliot leaves me at the bench, staring at Bishop in goal talking to Robicheaux and Kozlov, but with his eyes boring into me. A shiver runs down my spine as I lock eyes with him, and my tongue unconsciously slips out to wet my lips.

His mask is laying on top of the net, and he tries to look relaxed spraying water in his mouth as Robicheaux gestures animatedly to him. Kozlov stands to the side, resting the butt end of his stick on the ground, listening to Robicheaux, but clearly aware I'm there. Bishop says something in return, Roby shrugs, and the trio skate toward me.

"J-Lo! Hey girlie!" Roby calls out as he reaches me.

"Hey, Robes! Good practice?"

"Always! No such thing as a bad practice!"

"There will be when Mox tells you to run stingers," Kozlov intoned behind him, his accent thick. "Move, we're already late for team meeting."

"Alright, I'm going. See ya later!"

And then there was Bishop.

"Hello, Duchess. Getting into trouble already this morning?"

"I'm at work, Bishop. This is what I do."

He hums thoughtfully, stepping inside the door and latching it behind him. "Staring at me at practice is your work now?"

"I wasn't staring at you," I counter. "It looked like you were staring pretty hard at me though."

He shrugs underneath his pads, unrepentant. "Maybe. You were getting awfully cozy with Moxley."

"You mean the team captain who clearly has the hots for my best friend? Sure." I shift my stance under his unwavering gaze. "Why are you watching me so closely? Jealous?"

"No." One dark eyebrow lifts, before he glances around us, down the tunnel. Leaning in close, he whispers, "I can't stop thinking about last night."

"That makes work a little dangerous. Distractions in the goal?"

"I wouldn't say distractions, no." I feel my cheeks redden, and he smirks. "What are you doing tonight?"

"Two nights in a row?" Internally, I can feel my heartbeat in my throat. How the hell did he know that I had been hoping he'd ask that? "I don't have plans. It's a work night."

"Come over."

"I was just there," I counter.

"I know. I want to see you tonight."

"Are you getting clingy on me, Bishop?"

"I just want to see you again. I'll have dinner ready."

"That sounds like… a date."

Again, he answers the statement with a noncommittal shrug. "Come over, I'll send you the door code."

And without letting me protest further, he walks away, leaving me standing at the bench wondering what the hell just happened.

I CAN SENSE the chaos of the locker room around me, but I don't actually feel like I'm a part of it. All I can do is replay this week over and over again.

Never have I ever been obsessed with a woman before.

"Val, you good, man?" Elliot is standing in front of me, fully dressed for practice and staring at me, my laces loose, no shirt, just… sitting, staring blankly at the team logo.

"I'll be fine, just a lot on my mind."

"Do you want to talk about it? I'm here. You listened to me when I needed to talk about Ronni—"

"You think I'm having girl problems, Rookie?" I smirk, knowing that the nickname will get under his skin.

"No, but something is definitely under your skin, Old Man," he chirps back, and I roll my eyes before leaning forward to lace up my skates, with a crackle up my spine. *Maybe I am getting too old for this.*

"Let's go boys! The ice isn't going to get any better for you," Coach's voice bellows from the doorway, and I hurry to finish my prep work.

I've got to get Jessica out of my head but I'll be damned if

I can. And seeing her at the arena? In my locker room? It just makes everything from the weekend hit fresh again.

I step onto the ice, taking a lap or two to loosen up. I don't like that I take longer to do the things I used to do. Waking up the next morning after a game takes more effort than it did in my rookie season. I've watched Robicheaux curl into a little ball on the plane before, and it made my back twinge in sympathy. I haven't told anyone yet, but I wonder if I have another season under my belt after this. The more I work with the trainers, the more I feel like the answer is a resounding "no."

Stretching out in front of the goal, I do my best to tune out the surrounding conversations. I don't need to know who's banging who, or who's pissed that someone else got more ice time. I'm ancient in player years, and take longer to prep than before. I need to focus.

Moxley calls me "old man" as a joke, but it feels more like a fact than anything. I've contemplated hanging up my skates more than once in the last couple seasons, but I'm pretty sure this is going to be The One. The final season, the last ride. The farewell tour. Earlier in the season, I knew I needed to talk to my agent, get the ball moving to close the year. And I'd need to bring it up to Ronni and Jessica to see what team PR would want to do.

Jessica.

Just thinking her name made my heart race like someone coming at me on a breakaway. She's made a point of avoiding me as much as possible since the night I took her home from The Sin Bin. In the morning she left my house like a thief in the night, leaving me alone.

I'm the one that does the leaving, damn it.

She watches us warm up for practice at the bench, her ever-present tablet strapped to her wrist. Wrapped in an over-sized blue Ice Wolves Athletic Department hoodie, her warm brown gaze falls on me at the net, then to Robicheaux doing passing drills on the far side with Kozlov, and then bounces back to me. She's subtle. I doubt anyone else is noticing her. But I do. I notice everything when it comes to the ice and… her.

Moxley skates by her on a lazy arc, saying something that makes her laugh. "Show off," I grumble behind my mask, dropping back down into a defensive position and practicing some diving stretches to protect the goal. I can't let myself get distracted by her, no matter what.

"Bunch of useless fuckers," I growl to no one as the rest of the team gathers around her. "Hey, you ungrateful shits, are we practicing or having a circle jerk?" I yell, pulling my mask off.

"Aw, relax, it's for the fans," Roby calls back, grinning as he does something stupid that makes Jess laugh again.

I grit my teeth. This doesn't usually bother me so much, but today it's grating on my last nerve. Maybe it's because I'm tight and achy, and just want to make it into my massage appointment before my body gives out. Surely it has nothing to do with the fact that Jess has been invading my thoughts all day.

I'm not jealous. I don't get jealous. I'm just tired of the stupid little games that are keeping me standing here like an idiot–

A light check nearly takes me off my skates, and I glare at Moxley. I was so focused on Jess that I never saw him skate this way.

"If looks could kill, you would have just taken out part of my line," he chirps. "You good?"

"I'm fine, Just tired of waiting for whatever," I mutter. It sounded weak in my head, and even worse out loud. "Some of us have shit to do, ya know."

Moxley snags a nearby puck, skating in a loop around my net. My eyes zero in on the puck, watching his actions. The rest of the team, seeing him in motion, move into position, including Robicheaux. With one last glance toward Jess, I focus in on the players, the puck, everything that should be the center of my attention.

Game play, shot angles, unspoken calls between players. I claw my focus back to the game, cursing at my distraction. I need to be focused on giving this game everything I have.

Not gorgeous, dark haired temptresses leaving me alone in the middle of the night.

CHAPTER 12
JESS

MY PHONE SCREEN stares at me accusingly, the unsent text glaring at me in the harsh lighting. Yes, I know that phone screens can't actually have feelings or emotions, but I can feel it judging me.

> Me: What does a girl have to do to get you to come fold her like laundry?

I came home from work, ordered pizza, and immediately changed into my most comfortable clothes, sat down with my favorite bottle of wine and some trash television for background noise, and attempted to forget about that hot fucking goalie.

Three glasses of wine ago, I was perfectly fine ignoring how much I wanted him. I don't need to beg a man to come see me, I'm a big girl and I can take care of myself. I've had to handle this myself before.

Two glasses of wine ago, I contemplated the way he knew just the right button combo to make me come apart. Up, up, down, down, left, right, left, right, B, A, start button apparently has nothing on Bishop's skills. Someone should study him, because that was genius level work for the first time.

Last glass, I reopened the text I didn't send earlier. And now, as I look at my topped off glass sitting beside my laptop, I'm thinking maybe sending it wouldn't be such a bad idea after all.

Before my last remaining sober brain cell can tell me otherwise, I hit the dreaded button, watching the "Delivered" message pop up under the speech bubble. When it immediately flips to "Read 9:45pm," I scream, dropping it gracelessly on top of my foot.

"Fuck!" I screech, unsure if it's in response to the sharp pain in my foot or the near-immediate reaction from the man haunting my every waking thought.

Breath wooshes out of me as my cheery blue text bubble with the cheesy pick up line moves up, to be replaced by three flashing dots. He's responding.

"Shit, shit shit shit," I whisper. Excitement and horror battle inside me as the dots appear, disappear, and reappear.

> Bishop: Are you trying to seduce me, Duchess? Cute.

My gut drops. I expected him to answer, but cute? Like I'm some kind of puppy? It was stupid to think I'd be able to convince him to come over; I'm just the girl he sees at the club. Even if he did say he wanted a friends-with-benefits situation outside that private room.

I suck in a breath as my phone buzzes, flashing Bishop's picture under the incoming call alert. Closing my eyes, I blow out a long sigh, and press the green button before I can change my mind.

"Closing your eyes won't make me go away, Duchess," his disembodied voice purrs from my phone. I fling the phone against the throw pillow beside me. "Did you seriously just throw your phone? Come on, look at me." I can't move, all I can do is stare at my battered phone case sitting on the couch beside me. "Duchess…" His warning tone leaves no room for argument. Sighing, I reach over, pick up the phone, and slowly turn it over. He's apparently laying in bed, the dark pillows stacked behind him, his hair hanging loose across his bare shoulders. "Was that so bad?"

"I didn't expect you to video, I'm not really camera ready." I cringe, embarrassment heating my cheeks.

"Why do you say that, Duchess?" he asks, clearly looking around the screen, trying to see what I'm talking about.

Mortification has my stomach tied up in knots. He has never seen me at home, casual and not really fit for human consumption. I glance down at my threadbare, baggy college sweatshirt—the one that still has weird grease and food stains down the front of it from the last few hundred times that I've worn it. And my leggings. They've also seen better days, but they are some of the comfiest clothes. And he's asking to see this? You don't wanna see this, Sir.

I respond wordlessly, only by shaking my head. "I'm not even cute right now."

"I'll be the judge of that," he retorts. "Now flip your camera. I want to see your beautiful face again."

"Fine. But you asked for it," I grumble. Flipping the camera, I can still see my face in the small preview in the corner. I frown, groaning to myself as I look at my image next to his. He looks perfect, warm lighting, soft and golden. and his bare chest on full display has my mouth watering.

"That's my girl," he praises.

I roll my eyes, lifting a hand to smooth helplessly at the flyaways around my head. "You're so full of shit, Val."

"Don't disrespect my girl like that," he warns. "If I think you're beautiful, I'll say you're beautiful, and you know I don't bullshit."

In my gut, I know he's right because he has never pulled

punches with me before, if questions are dumb. He tells me questions are done if he doesn't like how something has looked on social media. He's even said it out loud at the moment. Lip service isn't something Bishop provides.

"You say that, though, but look at me." I loosely point in my direction. "I look like a troll—"

"You're comfortable, and that has nothing to do with beauty." He adjusts a pillow behind him, and resettles. "What are you doing tonight, Duchess?"

"Work stuff," I mutter, leaning forward to prop my phone against my water bottle, assuming the same position by my laptop that I had been in. "I had some last minute clips to clean up before tomorrow."

"That's not fun, working after hours. Did you text me to distract yourself? A little procrastination, perhaps?"

"Maybe." I open a fresh tab on my browser. "I kinda wondered if you would come over, but you don't have to, I mean, you probably have better things to do with your time. I'm sorry for bothering you."

"Duchess, you're spiraling."

I glare at the screen. "No, I'm not."

"You are," he argues with a laugh.

"I. Am. Not!" I yell back. With a huff, I reach over for my wine glass, taking a sip.

"How many of those have you had?"

"Just one," I hedge. No way I'm telling him it took the third glass to call him.

"I'm not fucking you if you're drunk."

I freeze. He's turning me down… I'm not worth it. I knew I was trying to girl boss too close to the sun pulling him. Yeah, he talks a good game at the club and all but I'm not that great.

"I wasn't serious, it was just a joke. I'm sure you're busy, I should let you go." I reach for the phone, preparing to end the call.

"Not so fast," he growls and I pause, my hand holding the phone away from me so he can't see my burning face. "I said I wouldn't fuck you if you're drunk, I didn't say I wouldn't come over. I'm just not going to put you into a position where you're not aware of consent. Now, flip this phone back over so I can see your gorgeous face." I open my mouth to protest, but bite the words back, instead doing as he says. "There's my girl," he praises, his voice doing that deep purr that makes my toes curl.

"You don't really mean that."

"I do. Now, you sent me an interesting message, and I want to know what you were thinking about."

I glance away, shaking my head. "You're really going to make me say it, aren't you?"

"What, that you were horny and you were trying to get me to come over and fix it for you? Yeah. I want to hear you say it. Tell me what you wanted." I look back to the phone to find his stare is unwavering. I chew on my lip nervously, unsure how to answer.

"I... I want you to come over."

"Because..." His tone is playful but with an edge to it.

"I guess because I wanted to see you." My cheeks burn, and I wait for him to admit he wants to see me too. He doesn't.

"Not good enough, Duchess. Give me more." Anger flares in my chest because this is not what I want.

"I'm not begging you, Bishop, so quit leading me on."

"Who said you needed to beg for anything? We're just talking."

"But I don't want to just talk." I huff in annoyance before adding, "It's just a waste of our time."

"Who knows where talking will lead us. You might be surprised." The silence hangs between us, thick and tangible even if we're in different spaces. "Tell me what you're thinking, Duchess, I need your words. And maybe if you can prove it isn't just the wine talking, then I'll reconsider. So again, tell me what you wanted when you sent your text. In detail."

I sigh, considering carefully just how much I want to say. I know what I want, and I'm a big girl and can use all my words. The idea that I can admit I want him, just for him to turn me down? I could never face him again, anywhere, not after he rejects me. My gut says he will; he was adamant about not being drunk when we're together. A slight buzz, sure, but that train left the station two glasses ago.

"I wanted you to come over, I'm lonely and I wanted to see you but now I'm just," I huff in frustration, "I'm embarrassed and feel like this is a joke to you and I'm just... I'm gonna go."

"Don't. I'm lonely too, and I'd love to see you. I like seeing you relaxed, even if you're technically working. We should do this together sometime, and I can bring over pizza. We can watch the replays for when Roby does stupid shit like falls over the boards."

I smile, remembering the footage. "He gave me content for weeks with that clip. So...game tape and chill? Is that how you get a girl's attention?"

"Not just any girl. You, though, I'd have to distract you from it I'm sure."

"Same for you. I've seen you with tape. You're hyper focused."

"Not this time. I think we'd be a mutual distraction. Could I get you to put your laptop away if I kiss that spot behind your ear again?"

My breath catches as I remember what that felt like. "Probably," I whisper.

"How would you distract me, Duchess?"

"I—" I clear my throat. "I'd straddle your thighs, block the TV with my chest."

"That would definitely work, I like how you think," he praises, looking down at his lap. "I can almost feel you there, warm and soft. I would run my hands up your thighs, under your shirt. What are you wearing under there?"

I blush again, looking away. "Um, nothing. I don't believe in bras or panties at home."

"Fuck, Duchess...." He sighs, sitting up in bed, tilting the camera angle as he goes. "Okay. I'll come over, but," he pauses, giving me a stern look, "if you're too drunk for my liking then I'm leaving. Got it?"

"I'm not, I promise! I'll send you the door code." We hang up, and I immediately panic. Am I too buzzed for him? "No, I only had a couple of glasses," I remind myself out loud. "After skipping lunch," I argue.

Shit. It's fine... I think.

"Ooh! Carbs!"

I run to the kitchen, hopeful that shoving a handful of cookies in my face will soak up some of the alcohol before he gets here. I continue through the house, half a cookie hanging out of my teeth as I run to hide my wine glass and partial bottle. Maybe I can just...

I top off the glass, then hide the empty bottle under a pizza box in my recycling bin, and go back for a sip. My phone dings, and I screech at the shock.

Bishop: On my way up.

"Shit, shit, shit!" How the hell did he get here so fast? I frantically wipe cookie crumbs off my face and sweatshirt, hoping I don't look as flushed and overheated as I feel at the moment. "Be cool, be cool, be cool," I mutter at myself as I walk toward the door, just in time to hear the solid thud of Bishop's fist against the wood.

I pause with my clammy palm against the knob, and peek through the peephole at a distorted Val Bishop, leaning one forearm against the doorframe, hair pulled back in his usual topknot, black hoodie clinging to his large shoulders.

"Fuck," I mutter.

"Are you going to open the door, Duchess, or just stare at me?"

Busted. Taking a deep breath, I open the door, coming face to face with him. The man walked across my lobby in grey sweatpants that did nothing to hide that he's half hard already.

"Are you going to invite me in?"

"Are you a vampire now?"

"If that's what you want," he chirps back. "I'm not afraid of a little role-play." He lifts his arm off the frame, prowling inside and shutting the door behind him softly, the click like a gunshot in the silence.

"C-come on in," I stutter, turning to walk toward the living room on shaky legs. How in the hell does just seeing him here unnerve me like this? He strolls into my space, making it feel small and claustrophobic as he looks around cataloging everything, before setting his gaze on me.

"I thought you said 'no bra or panties' at home," he comments, looking down at my leggings.

"I'm not answering the door with nothing on," I retort, crossing my arms over my chest defensively. "And what about you, those sweatpants are practically indecent."

"They hide what they need to. And considering what I wasn't wearing when you called... you're lucky I did this much. Now come here." I stumble over my own feet, cringing at my own clumsiness. He lifts an eyebrow in suspicion as I approach. "How much?"

The question hits me out of nowhere. "What?"

"How much did you drink, Jessica?" My heart races at my given name. Not Duchess. Not Jess. *Jessica.*

"I..."

"You know the deal. I told you before we hung up. What did I say?"

"You wouldn't fuck me if I was drunk," I mumble, gaze locked on my bare toes.

"And how much have you had to drink?"

"Just a glass…"

"Try again."

"I know what I'm asking for," I protest.

"I know what I said earlier, too."

"I'm not drunk, not really."

"Don't lie to me," he growls, but the tone only worsens the ache for him to touch me.

"I mean, I finished off my glass after—"

"Come on. You're going to bed." I start to sigh in relief until he finishes, "Alone."

"No!"

He walks toward my bedroom, leaving me to stare at his retreating back. He pauses, looking over his shoulder. "Let's go, Duchess, we don't have all night."

My head spins, trying to make sense of what is happening. He's here, in my house and we're what? Going to bed? To sleep? What the hell? "But what about—"

"Whatever you're about to say, it's going to wait for another night." He pivots and leans against my doorframe, crossing his arms across his chest. "You're going to bed, you're going to sleep this off, and we'll talk about this when you're sober."

I stomp my foot like a petulant child, and I can't even draw up the guts to be embarrassed about it. "It's not fair."

"What's not fair, that you sabotaged your own night? Duchess, this is just the consequences of your own actions. Now, let's go wash off your makeup."

Angry tears burn behind my eyelids as I cross in front of him to the bathroom. A large hand circles my wrist, pulling me up short so I have to face him. The action jars loose a tear, sending a hot trail down my cheek. "Hey," he says, softening his tone. "It's okay, I just want you clear headed when we play." The gentleness breaks me, just a little bit more. "It's not a 'no,' it's a 'not right now.' Okay?"

"I'm fine." I turn away from him, shuffling into the dark, turning on the bathroom light and reaching for the taps.

"Come here," he says, lifting me to sit on the counter by my hips, running his hands along my thighs. The quick movement catches me by surprise. "Let me take care of you. If you feel the same in the morning, we'll adjust." Making direct eye contact, he cradles my face, his thumbs wiping softly along the damp tracks. "You'll thank me later."

"Promise?"

"Promise," he whispers, placing a soft kiss against my lips, then on my tear stained cheeks. "Now let's finish up here so we can go cuddle."

"Cuddle?" The word feels strange on my tongue. "Did I hear you right?"

"Don't act so surprised, I can cuddle. You're not getting anything else from me." He pours a dollop of my facewash onto his fingertips, then snaps the lavender lid shut. "Now sit still, so I don't get it in your eyes." With the gentlest of touches, he massages the gel onto my skin. Once he washes away the remnants of the day he applies my toner and moisturizer like he knows my routine.

"You're a little too good at this facial treatment," I murmur, feeling drowsy as he loosens my bun, running my hair between his fingers.

"You forgot, I have a sister. Skin care was her obsession when we were growing up. And maybe I still have my own three-step process at home."

"That could be fun content," I reply with a sigh, leaning forward to rest my forehead against his shoulder.

"Hold on, Duchess, you're not done yet. Brush your teeth, and then we'll go to bed."

I finish like he said, exiting the bathroom to find him standing by the bed in his sweatpants and a t-shirt, hoodie hanging off my closet door, arms crossed. Without a word, he motions to the bed, the covers already turned down for us. Maybe…

"I can't sleep in this."

"So change for bed. I'll be waiting for you."

I smirk, grasping the hem of my hoodie and pulling it over my head. "Ooops."

"Duchess," he warns. "I don't reward brats. And I already told you, drunk is a hard limit."

"I know." I grab a t-shirt, throwing it over my head, before wandering over to faceplant onto my pillow. "You promised me cuddles," I demand, muffled.

He sighs, sliding in on the opposite side of the bed. "Come here, troublemaker."

Victorious, I slide under the sheets, leaning into his warmth, and allowing his thigh to sandwich between mine. I shift my hips, relishing in the feel of him.

"Don't think you can tempt me by humping my leg. The answer is still 'no' tonight."

Grumbling softly, I surrender for the night, letting his soft breaths under my head lull me to sleep.

———

My alarm cuts through my brain way too early and I remember in horrifying detail what happened the night before. Chugging wine. Bishop in my living room. Even worse, throwing myself at the man and hearing him say, "no." I swear on everything holy I'm never drinking again.

Bishop. Oh my God, he was here, and he put me to bed like a misbehaving child. Mortification turns my stomach. I'll never be able to face him again. Bracing myself, I roll over to find…an empty pillow.

"What the hell," I mutter, my voice dry and gravelly. Sitting up slowly, I glance around the room, seeing no sign of him, except for the massive hoodie hanging on my closet door.

I reach for my phone on the nightstand, finding a bottle of pain reliever on top of it and a bottle of water. I know I didn't put those there last night. The phone buzzes, turning the pills into a maraca. Sighing, I move the bottle, and look at the incoming message.

> Bishop: Morning, Duchess. Take the pills before you get out of bed. You'll thank yourself for it later. Sorry I headed out already, but I'll see you later.

So much for "we'll talk tomorrow," and "it's not right now," I fume, as I try to get up and mobile for the day.

CHAPTER 13

BISHOP

"ORDER FOR BISHOP," the barista calls out over the hum of conversation and light acoustic music from the overhead speakers. I wander over to them, mutter my thanks with a smile, and gather the drink carrier and steaming paper bags with my name scrawled on them. Hopefully, delivering some of my favorite hangover cures to Jess will make her feel better.

Cutting through the empty hallways of the arena, I replay the night in my head. The way she eventually opened up, telling me her thoughts. It was refreshing to hear someone be honest with me and not just give me lip service. However, I can't deny that I almost cracked and gave into the desire to touch her like she begged me, even if she didn't want to admit to doing that.

I find Jess at her desk, brows furrowed in concentration, beating the ever living tar out of her keyboard. My Duchess is pissed, and it's so damned adorable.

"Are you pouting, Duchess?"

"I don't pout," she bites out while continuing to type and not looking in my direction. She's so completely obvious, and it's actually adorable.

"Don't be like that, I told you what would happen. And one more thing, I brought you breakfast." I keep a teasing tone to my voice while waving the bag that has her favorite pastry just out of reach.

"That shit might work for Moxley, but I..." She pauses, looking sideways at the bag. "What's in there?"

"Chocolate swirl croissant filled with Nutella."

"Son of a bitch," she curses under her breath while leaning forward to graze her fingers against the white paper bag. "Fine, thank you for breakfast."

Finally.

"Forgive me?" I add-on, pulling the bag back just half an inch so that she can't get a proper grasp on it.

"I guess your reasons were sound, I'm just disappointed that you didn't cave."

"My reasons for breakfast aren't totally altruistic. I needed to make sure you had your strength up before you went to the conference room later."

"What are you talking about?" Her eyes narrow on me, suspicion darkening her gaze as she tries to calculate what I know that she might not. All of her emotions flash across her face and bright Technicolor, and I grin at how easy it is to read her

"You didn't know? We've got a new player coming in today. I don't know if anyone else knows yet; this kind of moved fast. But I'm supposed to go meet him and show him around, and I wanted you to tag along for pictures. He's gonna need a good intro because he comes with some baggage."

"Who did we get? I didn't hear of anyone on the trade block and I've had nothing show up about any changes to the social media calendar."

"You'll find out soon enough. See you in a bit."

I walk off before she can ask me any more questions, relieved that she doesn't seem to hold too much of a grudge.

———

This isn't my first time helping out when it comes to orientation with new teammates, but this is the first one that feels a little bit like I am pushing against the boundary between teammates and my friendships. I know there's bad blood between Kane Blackwood and Moxley, even if I don't know just how deep it is. I heard Moxley spent the morning yelling about punching him in the face again, and breaking his perfect nose again, to anyone that would listen. Whatever happened, it's definitely gotten under Moxley's skin and for the first time in a long time, I wish I could wear the C instead of him sitting in the conference room across from Jess. I try not to grind my molars into dust as the man in question, Kane, comes through the glass door and slides into the chair beside her and to the left-hand side of the commissioner. Normally, we sit on the right side of the table, and I expected him to take a seat next to me. Michael from public relations—Jess's boss—usually sits in that chair.

Despite the shake up in routine, I put a forced welcoming grin on my face. "Welcome to the team, Blackwood, I've heard a lot about your gameplay."

"Thanks, it will be good to not have to fight with getting a puck past your fat ass now," he chirps back and I can't help but laugh because it feels like he's going to be a great fit. It's a shame Moxley hates him so much, because he seems like a decent guy.

"It's great to have you on board, I wondered when I was going to be able to get that infamous pair back together again. The game tape of you and Moxley together was very impressive and I hope things haven't changed in the years since you joined the draft."

"I think we'll figure something out," Blackwood responds, his tone slightly cocky, but with the confidence that he'll back up what he's saying. Good luck to him, I think, as I look over at my girl, jotting down notes on her tablet and visually not paying attention to what's going on around her. I'm sure she's mentally checked in and picking up on everything we're saying, but I can't help trying to play.

Jess starts relaying schedules and ideas for getting updated graphics on the website and social media, and while she's distracted, I slide my chair slightly to the right. I'm curious how much she's paying attention to me, in all of this. She's tried to ignore me unless I am directly speaking with her, and she doesn't take the initiative to start anything with me. I slide my shoe across the midline of the table and wonder when I can find her. I know she has a tendency to sit with her feet out in front of her, legs straight and ankles crossed. That means I should find her right about...

Kane tilts his head, confused. He stutters out an answer to Jess and I watch her gaze drop from his face, down to under the table. She caught me. One dark eyebrow lifts in my direction. I retreat, giving her some space.

Conversations continue around the table and I offer ideas to get him acclimated with the team. Plans evolve to include content with Jess to pull her back into the conversation, so maybe she won't be suspicious anymore. Once I have her lulled into a false sense of security, I try it again. I make contact with the side of her high top, and cheer internally when she still doesn't react. I nudge my toe a little bit higher, watching her face for a reaction, when three things occur to me at exactly the same time.

One, that isn't her shoe.

Two, I'm rubbing up against Blackwood's ankle.

Three, she's pissed. The third thought only comes really clear to me when she kicks me in the shin—or at least I think it's her and not Blackwood kicking me.

"Fuck," I mutter, cringing as I feel my calf muscles start to complain and cramp. Despite the bad angle she started from, she made a direct hit.

"If you're done now, Bishop, perhaps you and Blackwood can go on a tour of the locker room." Jess's words are firm and commanding, and I shouldn't like it as much as I do. "It would be nice to get pictures of Blackwood with his locker so that way we can put it on social media," she adds as a professional courtesy.

"That's a fine idea," the commissioner adds on. "Welcome to the team, son, let's get you settled in and in some shades of blue instead of that god awful green."

JESS

BREATHE IN, *breathe out…*

I repeat the words in my head as I try to survive yet another nauseating wave of cramps. I shouldn't have come in to work today, but I had to get this report submitted before the weekend. Groaning, I double over in my desk chair and try to will the pain to stop.

"Jess, I can deliver that to Jerry when he comes through. Why don't you go home and relax? Curl up with your heating pad. There's nothing here that can't wait until tomorrow."

"I think I will," I reply, my voice muffled against my knees. "I can work on releases from home."

"Feel better, girl," she calls out, carrying my folder to her own desk.

The drive home is torture, but with every mile, I'm increasingly grateful for the potential rest at home. There are few things I hate in life: debilitating cramps are high on the list.

"Thank goodness," I sigh in relief, turning off the engine and slumping against the cool leather of my seat.

The walk to my apartment from the parking lot seems like

miles away, as I grit my teeth against the nausea roiling in my stomach. I just need to make it inside and then I can rest.

I visualize how it will feel, changing from the confining business casual apparel I put on this morning in favor of my oversized sweats. Shooting a weak smile at the older couple in the lobby, hoping I don't look as scary as I feel, I trudge to the elevator.

Just a few more feet, Jess, and you'll be done.

My keys rattle in my hand as I try to unlock my door. With a curse, I stab at the lock again, sighing as the metal slides home, taking away the last obstacle in front of me for the day. My purse lands in a heap near the table, the keys rolling off the mound with a halfhearted jingle, and I keep walking to my room, grateful for the soft click of the door settling back in its frame.

Home, finally.

My top lands in a silken heap near the hamper, the bra joining it on top, and I couldn't care less about the mess. The relief I feel as I unfasten my pants, the stiff fabric popping from the divots on my hips where it dug in all day, I could damn near cry. Throwing an oversized hoodie on with the sweatpants, I shuffle to the kitchen to make tea.

This better help.

Gingerly, I crawl into bed, my tea on my nightstand, my heating pad settled against my angry stomach, and hope to sleep off the rest of my cramps.

———

A pounding echoes through my apartment, jolting me awake from a sleep so deep I couldn't tell you what year it was.

"What the hell?" I grumble as I throw my bedding off, my heating pad bouncing on the floor at my feet. My ponytail flops limply against the back of my head, the band off-center and halfway down the length of my strands.

Thud-thud-thud.

"Keep your pants on, damn," I shout toward the front door, pulling my ponytail holder out of my hair and shoving a sleep-warm hand through the tangled mess. "So help me, if I'm doing this for a stupid salesperson," I mutter to myself, before stretching to look through my peephole at—

"Jess, it's Bishop. I know you're in there." His voice is muffled behind the wood.

"What are you doing here?" I ask, cracking the door open to peek into the hallway. There stands Bishop, wearing his usual gym gear, arms weighed down with plastic bags from a nearby grocery.

"Ronni said you went home sick."

My head rears back in surprise. Why would Ronni tell him that? And then, why would that mean he needs to show up?

"Yeah, I mean, I wasn't feeling that great earlier at work so she sent me home."

"Can you let me in? I think I'm about to lose one of the bags." I step back and hold the door open for him. He shuffles in, turning sideways to make it through the frame. "I'm going to put these in your kitchen."

"My kitchen— What? Bishop, what is all this?"

The plastic bags crinkle as they settle on my kitchen counter, and he makes quick work of sorting out the packages. I watch in awe as he stacks assorted soups, a loaf of sourdough bread, packets of cheese, and boxes of the electrolyte sticks he favors across the surface.

"Go lay back down, I'll have something ready for you in a minute."

"Bishop, I'm serious, what are you doing here?"

Large hands press down onto the counter as he stills, turning his head toward me. "Ronni said you went home, and you weren't feeling well. I went to the store to get you soup, and things to feel better, and I'm going to take care of you."

"Why soup?"

"She didn't say *how* you weren't feeling well, and soup just seemed… right."

My breath whooshes out of me in surprise. This giant man took it upon himself to get me comfort food because he thought I came home sick. "Um, Bishop?"

"Yes, Duchess."

"I didn't come home sick-sick. Um," I stammer, wondering how to talk to him. "I came home because I was cramping. Periods suck."

"And that makes a difference? You came home to feel better, the reasoning doesn't matter. Bacterial, viral, menstrual. You aren't well, and I'm taking care of you. I'm sure you haven't eaten anything since this morning, yeah?"

I blink in shock. "I didn't even really eat then," I answer softly.

His nods response is all I get for a moment.

"Well then. Like I said. Go back to bed, get comfortable. I'm heating this up and I'll bring it to you in a moment. Take a bottle of water with you. Your hydration habits suck."

His firm tone made me snort. "Yes, Daddy," I chirp back.

"And, Duchess?" I turn back to make eye contact with him as he begins pulling back his hair into a tie. "Don't earn punishments today when you'll have to cash them in next weekend."

ANGER SIMMERS in my chest as I pour the tomato bisque into a bowl centered on a plate with grilled cheese triangles around it. It isn't much, but it feels like comfort food will help. Hooking a mug of fresh tea with my fingers, I pick up the plate and head to her room.

Jess looks so small, curled on her side beneath her comforter, her iPad propped up against a pillow. She cringes as she shifts to sit up, and my anger resurfaces. Every goddamn month. She said it was like this every freaking month and does this alone. What kind of shit is that?

"Thanks, Bishop," she says softly, crossing her legs beneath the covers and settling the plate on top of her lap. "It looks great."

"It's just warmed up from the deli; it's nothing fancy. I just grabbed what was easy as soon as I heard."

"You really didn't have to. I'll be fine tomorrow. The first day just hits hard."

"I wanted to take care of you, Duchess." I smooth out the blanket around her calves. "I take care of what is mine."

"But I'm not, though."

"Not what?"

"Yours. We're friends with benefits, coworkers… whatever."

"Until we say we're done, you are mine. Don't doubt that for a single second."

She huffs, rolling her eyes. "Yeah, okay."

"You're not used to anyone taking care of you; being there when you need them. Am I wrong?"

"I'm a big girl, Bishop. Asking or expecting things from people leaves room for disappointment."

"Tell me what you need. Let me in."

"I'm just going to eat, turn on a comfort show, and then go to sleep." She sighs, breathing the steam from the bowl. "You don't have to stay."

"I'll stay until you're asleep and make sure the dishes are done. Deal?"

"Fine."

I watch her closely, a warm feeling in my chest as she slowly eats what I've given her as a reality show drones on in the background. I move the plate away when she's done, giving her space to get comfortable again. She shifts under the blankets, restless, moving the heating pad from her stomach to her back with a huff of annoyance.

"Can I do something that might help?" She freezes as my question hangs between us.

"Uh, sure."

"Set up your next show for us, then curl on your side so you're facing the screen." She does as she's told, the tablet propped against her lamp, and her back to me. I slide behind her, spooning her gently, holding the heating pad in place. Her sigh is music to my ears, and I feel her relax into my hold. "Better?"

"Much, thanks." She hums contentedly, and I smile into her hair, breathing that perfume that is all citrus and floral and her. In no time, her breathing shallows, her muscles relaxing as she settles into sleep.

I know I should leave her, like I said I would. This goes beyond our "friends with benefits" agreement. I don't stay to hang out, I don't snuggle, and for fuck's sake, I don't argue with myself over the need to sleep next to someone.

Moving slowly so I don't disrupt her, I slide out of bed. As I walk out the door after cleaning up, I can't help but notice an ache in my chest, and wonder when the hell that started.

———

My keypad chirps and lights up green as I unlock my door, and I let out a long breath, ready to welcome the peace and comfort of my own home. The heavy wood slides open, and I am assaulted by the sound of vocal fry and sobbing from my living room.

"What the fuck?" I mutter to myself as I step into the space and look around. I find my sister, sprawled in my living room, in neon, fuzzy pajama pants, and an oversized sweatshirt from my closet, her hair half in and half out of a bun. The floor around her is covered with the remnant of empty cheese puff bags, and there's a dripping tub of ice cream on its side, leaving a creamy trail across my coffee table. Her sobs are pierced by an annoying voice coming from my big screen that appears to be some reality TV show featuring a blonde woman in hysterics, screaming at a guy who looks like he wants to be anywhere else but there.

"What the hell happened here?" I ask from the doorway, afraid to step any farther in before I grind artificial orange cheese dust into my carpet.

Glancing up at me from her position on my leather couch, her mouth hangs open in shock. She reaches for the remote, turning the volume back down to a normal level, before turning back to me with a serious face.

"Bobby just broke up with Serena," she replies, as if I'm supposed to know who the fuck Bobby and Serena are.

I blink at her and then tilt my head. "And?"

"Bobby thinks it's too soon to commit and he doesn't want to hold her back, but it's really just guy-speak for he wants to sleep around so he's going to make it her problem." She tosses the remote down on the cushion beside her with a muffled thump. "Why do you guys always say that as if we want the freedom to sleep around, as if they are the one performing the charitable act by letting us go?"

"Well, not all guys..."

"I'm going to stop you right there, little brother. You may think you haven't done this, but everyone has pulled the 'let's just be friends' bullshit," she snarks with air quotes. "Even better, how about 'it's not you it's me,'" She adds in a mocking tone. "I swear to God, why does having a dick make everyone so goddamn stupid. You can have a perfect girl in front of you, the relationship is immaculate, and what do you do? You throw it all away on a chance that there might be something better out there that you could be missing. And you all wonder why there's a male loneliness epidemic."

"I'm sure it isn't as serious as all that," I try to add. "How about if you tell me why you're really here."

I watch on and horror as my stone-faced twin sister, the eldest of all my siblings by five minutes, crumples and resumes her sobs. I have no clue what to do or what is going on because this is not something that Vivienne Marie Bishop would ever lower herself to.

"Holy shit, Vivi, what the hell happened?" I tiptoe around some wayward cheese puffs and make my way to the couch beside her. Her arms wrap around me with lightning reflexes, and I struggle to breathe against her boa constrictor embrace.

"He cheated on me. I caught him in our bed with someone else."

"I'm going to fucking kill him," I growl, anger flaring in my veins at how her stupid boyfriend treated her.

"I had to leave; I couldn't stay there anymore. He didn't even apologize, he just said he needed a moment to make sure he wanted to commit."

"And he thought slipping his dick into somebody else was going to give him that kind of clarity?"

"Apparently. I thought I would go back and we could talk about it, but he just told me today that he's taking my name off of the lease and he's shipping my things back here." She sniffles against my shirt, and I cringe at the wet sound of it. "I gave him your address because I didn't know where else to send it to. I'm going to go look for my own place this week, I just couldn't do it today."

"Stay here as long as you need. There's plenty of space." I feel the tension leave her body, and she slowly pushes off of my chest to sit back. Her bun flops to one side, a tendril of hair getting caught on her damp cheek, and she swipes at it.

"You're the best, V, you know that, right? I don't know where I would be without you"

"Sitting in Southern California trying to beg some two-timing loser to take you back?" I ask with a shrug. "Don't you fucking dare go back to him. Just stay here, and if you want your own place, I'll help you settle in. There's supposed to be a couple new vacancies here in the building so you can just go a floor or two down."

She chuckles humourlessly. "I'm sure they would love to rent out to an unemployed actress/waitress/virtual assistant who can't even keep a boyfriend around."

"When you tell them I'm your brother, they won't be an eyelash. It'll be fine. And honestly, I would rather have you someplace safe. I know the security here; they'll take great care of you and I'll be nearby if you need anything."

We look around at the aftermath of her post breakup pity party, and she sighs deeply. "I'll get this cleaned up, and then if you don't mind, I'm going to go take advantage of your wine fridge, and your hot tub."

"Make sure you drink some water in between, and don't die in there."

I make my way into my office where the bottles of perfume are still lined up across my desk. I pick up the one that I now know belongs to Jess, and tuck it away in my drawer. I fire off a text to let Conway know to take these back to the store as well, and relax back into the leather chair.

HANGING out with Viv on a Wednesday night should be peaceful and relaxing. Instead, I'm scrolling through old texts with Jess, and anxiously waiting for a new one to appear. "So damn needy," I grumble. "She doesn't even know you want to talk."

"Your face is gonna freeze that way if you don't stop it," Viv calls out from the other side of the couch, nudging me with a bare toe, and then throwing popcorn at me.

"Gross, Viv," I grunt, shoving her foot away. "You're such a child, I swear."

"I'm five minutes older than you, and you know it."

I roll my eyes, knowing she's just trying to antagonize me into answering. "I'm fine."

"You don't look fine," she counters, sitting up crosslegged to face me. "You look pissed about something."

"Just waiting on a text, that's all."

"Is it from a girl?" she sing-songs, and I try not to throw a pillow at her. I'm a grown-ass man, I'm bigger than that.

"Maybe. None of your fucking business, either way."

"It is!" Her eyes go wide as she leans forward on her knees. "Tell me more. I want to know all about her. Where did you meet? What does she look like? Oh! Can I meet her?"

"Jesus, Vivienne, take it down a notch."

"You never get this worked up over a girl, so excuse me for being excited about it."

"I'm not, so…"

"You are too," she taunts.

"What are you, twelve? It's not that serious."

"For 'not that serious,' you look stressed about it."

"Oh my God, for the last time, we're just…" I open my hand in front of me, like the correct words will just fall out of the sky, and then sigh. "We're just hooking up."

"You don't put this much effort into someone you're just fucking, Val, and you know it."

I refuse to admit that she might be right.

"Tell me the last person you stared daggers into your phone over that wasn't part of the coaching staff." She cocks an eyebrow. "I'll wait."

"You're ridiculous," I grumble, glancing at my phone for the millionth time. "I'm going to bed, I have early practice in the morning. When is your meeting about your apartment again?"

"Tomorrow at noon. Thanks for that, by the way."

"Anytime. Night," I call over my shoulder, heading to my room with way too many thoughts buzzing in my skull.

Two days later, my sister's words keep bouncing around in my head, the phrases ricochet off of my oversized thoughts.

Are you sure you don't have feelings for this girl?

You don't put this much effort into someone you're just fucking, Val, and you know it.

I shake my head forcefully, trying to dislodge her voice. She's wrong. I always take care of the people around me. I have always made sure my partners receive proper aftercare. I make sure my teammates are in a good headspace after losses or before major games. I check in with them when they're off the roster for healing and I show up to see them when they feel like everybody else has forgotten them, wrote them off for the season.

It grates on me how close to the truth she got. I never do sleepovers and what did I do the first time I hear that Jess just isn't feeling like her normal self? I go full Overbearing Daddy and take care above and beyond. It's almost like I'm trying to be a boyfriend, who the fuck does that?

I shouldn't be dwelling on this right now as I prepare before the game. My headphones drown out the cacophony of the locker room, and I allow my eyes to shift out of focus. It's the same thing I do every game, I never divert from routine. Why does this feel different? Instead of envisioning saves and game strategies, visualizing shot angles and body language of the opposing team, I'm instead focused on wondering what that dark-haired temptress is up to, as if I don't know. I just passed her half an hour ago in the tunnel.

My mind wanders again, seeing what it would feel like for her to wait for me after the game, riding home together.

No. We're just scratching an itch. It's not that serious.

I SHOULDN'T BE USING my time building social media posts as an opportunity to eye-fuck my situationship, but here I fucking am. It's only been a week since I last saw him away from the arena, so why am I such a mess today? I pick up my phone, open our text thread, and start to type a "what you doing?" then slam my phone back down on my desk in disgust.

Jesus, Jess, can you beat any thirstier? Focus on your damn job.

Annoyed with myself, I start rearranging the images within the blog post about the "top five plays of the week" all over again, trying to avoid the two picture perfect saves with that particular goalie. There's plenty of time for discussing my next hook up with Bishop after work. Just thinking his name sets loose the mental instant replay of him, pressing me against the wall and running his hands up my–

"Jess? Are you okay?" I squeal, jumping in my seat, and staring wide eyed at Ronni. "Do you need to take a minute? You're looking a little off."

"No, I'm fine. I just need to get this done."

"Well, I'm going to run over to The Den and get some coffee. Do you want one?

That would be amazing. Thanks, girl."

She wanders off, leaving me in the office alone. I pick up the phone again and start to type out another message, and groan as I put it back down, sliding it to the far corner of my desk space.

"Oh my fucking God, his dick isn't magic!" I mutter under my breath to myself.

"Really? That's not what you were telling me last week." Bishop's sultry voice has my thighs clenching.

"Aren't you supposed to be at practice?"

"They're working with Woody. I had other plans."

"Harassing me at work?"

"Hardly, Duchess. Although it feels like I'm the one being harassed. Talking about my cock at work, what would HR say?"

I stare him down, panic blooming in my chest. "Don't. Start."

He looks around casually. "Everyone's out of the office, right? No one will know."

"You don't know that!" I hiss quietly.

"Ronni just walked away. Michael's office door is closed. The interns are chasing around the rookies. You're on your own, Duchess, it's fine."

I take a slow breath, calming my nerves. "If we get caught..."

"We won't."

"You don't know that. And you might be able to smile and get away with this, but I can't!"

"Hey," he says softer, soothing even. "We're just coworkers talking, okay? We do this all the time. I tell you stupid social media trends I saw, and you tell me when we're going to do them. Business as usual."

I shake my head, of course we can have a reasonable conversation without being guilty. "You're right..."

"I usually am." At his cocky grin, I roll my eyes. . "So, you were saying…"

"You're determined to get this back to a not-safe-for-work conversation."

"You're the one thinking about my dick, not me. So, do you want to come over tonight?"

"Will it make you walk away from my desk before someone asks what we're talking about?"

"Maybe," he responds, grinning widely. "See you at seven?"

My face grows hot as I nod, waving him away as I hear Michael's door opening. "That was close," I mutter to myself, watching Bishop disappear around a corner before anyone can see.

———

Approaching Bishop's door feels natural, and not like we're hiding. No one bats an eyelash as I walk across the lobby, enter the elevator, and head to his floor, as ifI've done this a thousand times. I barely get my knuckles against the dark wood before the door opens, and Bishop's hand grabs my wrist, pulling me inside.

"Jesus, what the–" I start, only to be cut off by his mouth fusing to mine, melting my protests before they can form. His touch is everywhere, and with the frantic way he's pulling at my clothing, I don't think we're making it past the living room.

"Need you now," he growls into our kiss. He walks us blindly into his space, pressing the backs of my thighs into his dining room table.

"Here? Really?" I ask, breathless, as he presses me back onto the glossy surface.

"It's my table and my woman, I'll do what the fuck I want."

Why the hell is that so hot?

He makes quick work getting my panties out of the way, sliding a condom on at record speed. "No foreplay?"

"I've been hard since I left your office hours ago, thinking of sinking myself inside you. We're going to be at this for hours, Duchess. You're not going anywhere." My whimper turns into a moan as he drives into me in one smooth thrust. "Feels like you've been thinking about it just as long, too. Have you been wet for me all afternoon?"

"Maybe– fuck!" I curse as he swirls a thumb around my clit. "Not fair how good you are at that."

Making eye contact with him should feel too intimate, too much like–*don't even think it*–for as casual as we are, but I can't stop myself from gazing up, and finding him locking in on me. I can't help but feel something as he changes his angle slightly.

"That's my girl, you're taking me so well," he praises, and it's all I need. I shatter, feeling myself tighten around him, even as I close my eyes against the pleasure and breaking that link with him. He continues thrusting, coming with a grunt before leaning down to kiss me.

"That was…" I don't even know where I thought I would go with that, I have no words for what it feels like with us.

"I know," he answers, pressing a kiss to my collarbone. "We'll go slow next time."

"Next time?" He leans up, making eye contact with me.

"You don't think I invited you over to bang you for five minutes on my dining room table, did you?" I giggle at his incredulous tone. "I'm not done with you, that was just taking the edge off." He presses kisses against my throat, making me purr contentedly in his hold.

"You're good at that one," I murmur, turning my head just enough to place a kiss on his hairline.

"God, I missed you," he whispers, peppering kisses along my collarbone.

"Bishop, the doorman sent me up with– Oh, my God!" A woman's voice calls from the entry way. Panic seizes me, adrenaline pumping through my veins as I start to fight Bishop off of me.

"Viv, what the fuck?" Bishop roars, trying to cover up what little exposed skin we had, fighting to get his jeans back into place.

Viv? Who the hell is she?

"Oh my god *my eyes*!" She screeches, dropping a box inside the doorway, slapping her hands over her face. "Jesus, cover your pasty ass at least, that's so gross! What happened to the hair tie on the door handle warning? You're paying for my eye bleaching!"

She doesn't move, she just stands there, yelling at Bishop, and I do the only thing a reasonable woman would do in this situation.

I run.

I DON'T HAVE *time for this.* I growl to myself as I look across the season ticket holder event at the one and only Val Bishop giving me moon eyes and trying to motion me to go down a hall.

What the actual fuck, dude?

Rolling my eyes at his insistence, I step towards Ronni, who is already talking to some of the season-ticket representatives about the plans for the evening. I give her some bullshit excuse that I need to go run to my desk for another box of fliers, then make my way to where he is still lurking. Crossing the threshold between the open space of the concourse and the side passage that goes toward meeting spaces, I let my customer service face fall. Masks off, gloves off, he's gonna hear about this. Watching his broad shoulders ahead of me, I feel my blood pressure rise with each step that he takes, and I can't even enjoy the view of his ass in those well tailored dress pants right now. It's an absolute waste, I think, because I'm going to strangle him as soon as I get him alone.

His stride slows, allowing me a chance to catch up. He casually glances around, looking behind me, before he reaches out and snatches my wrist, pulling me into the darkness.

"I didn't think he was ever going to stop talking to you," he growls, pressing me against the door, before his hungry lips descend onto mine.

My hands slide into his thick hair, tugging in the way I know that he likes, but also to pull him away, so I can talk. "I have a job to do, Bishop, I can't just be in here, sucking face with you," I hiss at him, trying to keep the volume down in case anyone walks down the hallway. I can't help myself as I pull him back to me and kiss him back hungrier and harder than he kissed me.

He grunts against my assault, but counters, picking me up by my thighs with his strong hands, so I straddle his waist, before turning to walk me towards the table.

"I've been dying to do this to you all goddamn day," he mutters against my lips, pressing my knees apart and greedily running his fingers over the lace of my panties. "You wore my favorites?"

"Fuck your favorites, they're mine. Did you have to drag me in here like a caveman?" I whimper as he drops to a knee in front of me, pulling the scrap of fabric down my legs and stuffing them into his jacket pocket. "I'm getting those back before we leave, don't get too attached."

"We'll see about that." He leans forward, dropping open mouthed kisses against my inner thighs, edging closer to my center. "Color."

"What?"

"What color? Are you in this with me or not?"

"Jesus, Val, green. Quit dicking around and fuck me already."

He pauses, looking up at me with one eyebrow quirked. "If you insist, but just know I'm going to feast on you for hours later."

"We don't have time for this." I moan, grasping onto his lapels. "Gonna get caught."

"Maybe we should get caught, then everyone can know you're mine." He makes quick work of his belt and zipper, running his bare length against my clit. "Let everyone see how well you take me."

"Quit teasing me and do it," I say against his lips. "Please."

"You know I love it when you beg for it." He presses his blunt head against me, pausing. "Shit, condom."

"No time. I'm on the pill, we're both tested, just do it already."

"You're killing me, Duchess," he groans, thrusting forward. "God, you feel so good."

My head drops back against the wood, and I just hold on for the ride, listening to his litany of filth.

"I should send you back out there without your panties. What would everyone say if they knew you were out there, bare ass with me dripping down your thighs?"

Without saying a word, I wrap my legs around him, pulling him tight against me, impossibly deep. "Dare you," I taunt, grinding against him. "I don't think you'll do it."

"Watch me," he counters, placing a hand over my mouth. "You need to be quiet, though." I nod my agreement, and he grins, biting his bottom lip before slamming into me.

My eyes roll back in my head, toes curling, and all I can do is ride the waves of my orgasm. Stars explode behind my eyelids, and I feel his rhythm falter. He's close, and just thinking it ramps me closer. He pulls his hand back from my mouth, pressing his fingers against my clit.

"Are you going to come for me? Make me a mess," I cut off on a moan, his fingers sending shockwaves through me. "Need to feel you, please."

"Damnit," he curses. "Not until you do. Come for me, Duchess." His words, his touch, his everything, sends me over the edge, setting off a chain reaction. "Holy shit," he breathes, leaning down to kiss me.

I don't understand the magnetism between us. Why can't we be in a room alone together without spontaneously combusting? As my breathing slowly catches up, I feel panic rise in my chest. What the hell have we done? At work? Where anyone can catch us?

"Get up," I whisper, trying to push his bulk off of me. "We need to stop and get out of here." He hums in agreement against my neck, without moving.

"I know," he murmurs into my neck, kissing me lightly before standing upright, leaving cool air and goosebumps in his absence, before helping me sit upright. Cradling the sides of my face, he leans in for another kiss.

"Bishop. Yellow." He freezes, before stepping fully back.

I shift off the tabletop, careful to get my footing and trying not to leave a trace of us on the glossy wood beneath me. So damned reckless of us.

"God, I need to go back out there before they know I'm gone," I hiss, trying to smooth out my clothing. I look around frantically, where the hell are my... "Panties. You're not keeping them."

"Duchess, just a minute, okay–"

"I don't have a minute, and I'm not going out there without them. Not today."

"Okay, here you go," he says, sliding them out of his pocket. "Can we talk first? I've been trying to get your attention all night."

"Well, you've got my attention. What do you need?" My arms crossed, protectively across my chest, and I brace myself for whatever's going to come out of his mouth.

"We need to talk," he answers, his tone, soft, compared to normal. I'm taken aback, so accustomed to him being take-charge, in command, dominating the conversation.

"So, talk." I grimace at the tone that just came out of me.

"I'm sorry, but you have had so much time to talk before now and I'm kind of busy, and frankly the hot and cold is making my head spin."

"I know. I honestly don't know where to begin, or how to make things right again. Things have felt really weird between us and I want them to go back."

"Back to what? Back to when I was just the social media girl, and you ignored me half the time? Back to when I was your little plaything in the club? This wasn't supposed to be anything serious, and in the past two weeks you have bounced back-and-forth between boyfriend and friends with benefits. Make up your mind."

"Jess, I'm sorry I didn't mean to throw your mixed signals. To be honest, it has confused me, too."

I just stare at this giant of a man, hands stuffed in his pockets and scuffing the toe of his loafer against the floor. His posture feels more like a kid getting lectured for being out after curfew, as opposed to the confident man I've known for years.

"So, where is your head right now?" I cross my arms tighter across my chest on instinct, not even caring about the body language training that told me this poster wasn't helpful in a conversation. Fuck that. Dude can grovel and deal with it.

"I don't know if I have an answer for that. I mean, you were right, I have a reputation of being a fuck boy, but I'm tired and honestly, seeing some other guy talk to you just does things to me and I know I don't have a right to feel these things but I do. I want to change my image and I want to keep you at the same time. I don't know if I have the right to even tell you what to do."

"I can guarantee you do not have the right to tell me what to do. If you ask nicely, we can discuss, but you're not going to tell me a damn thing here, Bishop. I'm at fucking work."

"I know. And," he sighs, "I know how this looks. I just, I feel like we can be so much more than—"

"Than what? Fuck buddies?" An incredulous laugh erupts from me as I look at his offended face. "Look, I knew what we were when we started, okay? Don't try to force something that you don't want."

"But I do want—"

"Bishop. Stop. Just because you've stayed interested in the same person for more than a month, doesn't mean you have to commit." Against my better judgement, I drop a hand on his large forearm, enjoying the bunch and release of his muscles. "I know the rules. You don't have to worry about me catching feelings." His shoulders drop slightly, and my heart beats off-kilter at the look of defeat tightening his jaw. The tension still hangs between us, and without a moment to second guess myself, I step forward on my tip toes and drop a kiss against the corner of his mouth.

"Come home with me tonight," he demands, the commanding Bishop I'm used to returning.

"But your sister…"

"She has her own place now."

"And this is just…"

"It's whatever you want it to be. I'm"—he breathes in—"I'm whatever you want me to be, when you need it. If I'm just a dick you dial occasionally, that's what I'll be."

I SHOULD HAVE EXPECTED that I wouldn't just be able to leave Bishop behind. It was bad enough that it took over a week for me to not choke up smelling his cologne, or hearing his voice. Seeing him on ice still borders on torture. Between the warring feelings of what we do, and the mortification of his sister walking in on us, I can't even begin to untangle the mess of emotions I have.

"You're her, aren't you? The one saved in his phone as Duchess."

I jump, my scattered thoughts distracting me from the world around me, and look into the eyes of a person I can only describe as the more feminine version of Bishop. She's several inches taller than myself, but the same dark hair is back in a ponytail. Her features are still striking, like his, but with a softer edge to them, her lips work into a smirk that reminds me of the one he delivers during a well-placed chirp during interviews.

"I don't think we've met," I start, trying to be pleasant with a stranger, but not liking how familiar she is with information that Bishop told me would stay private.

"I knew it," she practically shouts, the smirk brightening

into a grin. "I'm his sister, Vivienne. Sorry for busting in on you guys the other night, he wasn't expecting me." Her cheeks go crimson as she looks down at the floor, embarrassment all over her face. "I really should've called him before I just dropped in, but I really didn't expect him to be home, like, at all. He never stays there."

"It's okay, I shouldn't have been there anyway. It won't happen again." I moved to excuse myself from this awkward conversation, when she latches a hand on my wrist.

"Yeah, that's what I came to talk to you about. I think you're good for him. He rarely lets people in and I've worried about him a lot. He honestly isn't the same anymore, and that's a good thing. He's happy now—less of an asshole."

"How can you tell that? He's like talking to a brick wall sometimes."

Vivienne glances down at her hand, twisting a stack of rings around her index finger. "I know he's not a big talker with his feelings; he's always been that way. But it's in the way he acts. I mean, I heard the man went over to your place to take care of you. Respectfully distanced, waited for word about what they'd need, but to dive full-on into caring overnight? You're special to him."

I roll my eyes, not buying it. "It was a lucky guess. He stopped to see me and Ronni told him I went home sick."

"He's never, in the history of ever, done that for a woman he's dated, or even his closest friends. Hell, we went to college together, and that wasn't something he would do without explicit instructions. Even for me, and I'm his twin."

My forehead creases as I think it over. "It's cute and all, but you know we're not serious, right?" I cringe internally, grasping at the words to make this less awkward. "I mean, we're not dating. I'm not his girlfriend, we're... we're..."

"Occasionally hooking up? Booty calls? Friends with benefits? Just fucking? Yeah, I know. He doesn't do serious relationships, or never has in the past. But I think he's trying to change that."

"But… why?" The question slips out of my mouth before I can even fully form it in my brain. I freeze, looking at her, mortification dripping cooly down my spine. I press on. "I mean, why now? Why me? I'm not his usual type."

"Honestly? TWell, that might be it. I mean, look at some of his past dates to galas and whatnot. Who were they, really?"

"Nondescript eye candy that he never remembered their names for photo credits." An ember of anger reignites as I remember trying to track down their names for social media after events. Val sitting on a bench in the locker room, a shrug of his large shoulders and muttering, "I don't know, I just met her," before trying to change the subject.

"Exactly. But with you… I don't know if you realize how often your name is in his mouth. He sees something that needs to go on socials, he wants to know what you'd think. He took me to a cafe around the corner from the apartment and he made a second order just for you because he thought you would like it. I mean, he's probably a couple smiles away from tattooing your name on his body, for goodness sakes."

"That's a commitment," I mutter, and while I keep my face neutral, the butterflies in my stomach multiply dangerously.

"Don't ice him out," she responds, her tone almost pleading. "I know we just really met, and you don't really know me, but just think about it, okay? He's really trying."

I nod my head, noncommittally, and hate the guilt that sits heavy in my chest when her face lights up, so eerily similar to his. "I'll try."

"Good. I hope we can meet up again soon, I think we could be great friends," she responds, and in a very un-Val-like move, wraps me in a hug. "Talk soon, yeah?"

CHAPTER 20

BISHOP

FUCK. This. Shit.

She thinks I can't have a serious relationship? Just because I've never been in one, doesn't mean I can't do it. I've never actually been on a line with Moxley, but damnit if that's what I needed to do I'd figure it out.

Scrolling through my phone on a plane to our next away game netted me next to nothing as far as ways to prove I'm serious. Committed to the cause. This couldn't be that complicated if everyone else around me could function. I mean, if Bryant Fucking Tudor from the Tallahassee Gators could manage to not only secure a relationship with a woman but also create four clones of his thumb-headed self, I can do it. I may be a goalie, but I'm not as weird as that fucker.

Kids. Damnit, now all I can see is my penthouse with miniature versions of myself, lanky boys playing mini stick hockey in the hallway and an eagle-eyed girl that looks just like Jess blocking her brothers' shots, delivered with a scathing chirp that would make other hockey moms cry. Everyone living in the past would think the boys were carrying on my legacy, but it would be her. There is no way in hell I would leave my girl riding the pine; she'll play just as well as the boys. I just know it.

And Jess would be gorgeous and curvy with my child, her edges all soft in pregnancy. I could see her in my living room, feet propped up on the couch, her laptop in front of her little basketball belly, building social media posts while I watch my game tapes with her. My breath escapes on a harsh exhale and did I— Oh my god, I've gone from permanent bachelor to breeding kink in point-six seconds.

She's going to fucking kill me.

I shake my head like I can visibly knock away the invasive thoughts, the force knocking my hair into my eyes. Get your shit together, Bishop. First things first, establish the relationship.

How can I convince her that I'm serious, that I'm in this for the long game, that I'm tired of playing the field? Taking care of her when she didn't feel well wasn't enough. Or, maybe it would have been, but she still doesn't see it as a permanent thing.

I sigh in disgust, scrolling through stupid articles titled, "Top 10 Gifts for the Woman You Love," hoping to find something that suits Jess.

"B, buddy, I think your phone case just cracked in your hand." Elliot's voice in my ear makes me jump, flinging the offending piece of technology to the carpeted floor at my feet.

"Motherfucker," I curse, trying to fish it out from under the seat in front of me, knowing there's no way in hell I can fold small enough to get it off the floor.

"Woah, dude, let me get that… there ya go," he says, kneeling in the aisle and picking up my phone, watching as the screen lights back up and instead of showing my nondescript wallpaper… "Top 10 Gifts for… B, you're in love?"

"Shut up," I grumble, snatching my phone away. "It's probably a stupid pop up ad or something."

"No, don't think so, buddy. So, who is she?" His stupid

golden retriever face is locked on mine, his equally stupid grin unshaken by my frown. "I won't tell if that's what you're worried about. I mean, I know you keep your private life, well… really, really private."

I sigh. He won't let this drop. Even if I distract him now, he'll remember later. Maybe at the hotel if I'm lucky, but knowing him, he'll wait until the locker room when I can't escape.

"If I tell you, I mean it, you can't tell anyone. Especially not Ronni."

"Not a problem. Let's do this."

"It's Jess."

"Wait, *Jess* Jess? Like, Ronni's best friend Jess?"

I nod my head slowly, looking around the plane at the rest of our teammates to see if anyone else is listening.

"Holy shit, dude," he whispers in awe. "How did that even happen?"

"What do you mean 'how did that even happen,' like how did you and Ronni happen?"

"Oh, I had to wear down her defenses. She hated my guts," he answers with a laugh. He's close to the truth, she really didn't like him in the beginning.

"She thinks I'm not serious."

"You're the most serious person I know. You never pause, you're like a machine."

"Not that," I grumble. "She thinks I'm not serious about starting a real relationship."

"Well, are you?"

"What kind of stupid question is that, Mox? Of course I'm serious."

"Okay, got it. It's just," he pauses, "no one has ever seen you with a girlfriend, nothing long term. So, how long have you been dating her, then?"

"We haven't really–not officially, anyway."

"So ask her out and make it official. What's the issue?"

"She thinks it's just casual, and that's all it will ever be." His bark of laughter turns heads our way, and I smack my hand against his chest. "Shut up! I'm serious. I've never had a serious relationship in public so she thinks I won't commit."

"So fix it."

I roll my eyes, staring him down. "Do you think I haven't tried? She maintains we're just friends with benefits, and that it's what she's happy with. She deserves more, and I can give her so much more, it's just…" I grunt, looking down at the phone in my hand. "I guess, I just really haven't had to do that before."

"Haven't what?"

"Give someone more before. A fun night out here, a moment there, but never–"

"Bishop. Buddy, are you saying you've never had a *girlfriend* before?"

"Don't be a fucking asshole," I grumble. "Maybe it's been a while."

"Bishop's having girl troubles?" A disembody voice called from a nearby seat. I look around and find one of our veteran forwards, peeking over the top of my seat back, his eyes and nose just visible over the top of the cushion, "Buy her a gift or take her on a trip, it works for my girl every time."

"I didn't even know you had a girl," Moxley chirps back at him.

"Oh, I don't right now, but I did. Last season. You didn't meet her."

"So tell me again how that worked to make her happy." The jab leaves my lips before I can think, feeling disgruntled that people are interjecting into a private conversation that I didn't even want to start to begin with.

"It worked because she was happy until she figured out I was gone more than I was ever home. She was great, but I think this life was a little much for her."

"She's a workaholic so sending her on a trip probably will

not do it," I muse, frowning, and thinking about things she might like. I know nothing about her outside of work and our occasional hookup. "Maybe a proper date is a good place to start."

———

Road trips used to be fun and exciting. Now, all I want to do is go home and lay in my ridiculously expensive orthopedic bed and hold my girlfriend.

Girlfriend? Where the hell did that come from?

I try to stretch out on my hotel bed, gritting my teeth in annoyance as I start to feel a telltale twinge in my lower back that says that this is not going to be my night. The trainers are going to have a fit tomorrow when they try to loosen me up before the game. I need a distraction. Before meeting Jess, I would have looked into the nearest burlesque show or club and spent a few hours there, enjoying the ambience, but now without her by my side, it doesn't feel right. The clock on the nightstand table shows six o'clock here on the West Coast, which means it's nine for Jess. Technically, it's not too late to call her, but would she talk to me?

Before I can second-guess myself one more time, I press Jess' name for a video call and wait.

"Hey! How's the weather in San Jose?" she answers on the second ring, and I feel something in my chest loosen as she smiles at me.

"Perfect as always," I drawl. "It's about the only thing it has going for itself here."

Jess shifts her position, the phone settling a little farther away, so I can see more of her. The living room and her apartment with the vivid movie posters on the wall behind her is a familiar and welcomed sight. My heart aches a little, and it feels nearly like home sickness. She's sitting on her couch, her hair thrown up into a messy bun with pencil sticking through it. The Ice Wolves sweatshirt she's wearing hangs precari-ously with the neck line about to slide off of his shoulder, the raw edge cut wide to show off her collar bones. If I could, I'd dress her like that every fucking day but in a sweater with my name on the back.

Since when are collarbones sexy?

"What are you doing, Duchess?"

"Prepping your pregame posts. The social media machine doesn't stop just because you have an away game."

I just pause, watching her lean forward to type something on her laptop, her eyes gleaming as she puts the finishing touches on the screen in front of her. Pride swells in my chest as I watch her in her element, in her natural state. "Has anyone ever told you how hot it is to see you work?" The words escape, unbidden, and I have a moment of panic as she freezes, then side eyes me.

"Has anyone told you that you need to get your vision checked in your old age?" She wrinkles her nose and looks at me straightforwardly. "I've already taken my contacts out, my makeup off, and I look like a mess. Your words are bullshit and I know it."

"You have no idea what this look does to me, do you?" She shakes her head, not believing a word I've said. "How much more time do you need for work?"

"I was just about done for tonight, then I was going to go take a bath."

"Oh really…" *Well, this phone call just got interesting.* "Take me with you."

"Do I look like a cam girl to you?"

"Right now, yeah. Go run your bath. Duchess. It's time for you to relax."

"Yeah, yeah, you just want to see me naked."

Her sassy response has me lifting a brow at her. "That was bratty."

"So you're just going to what, sit there like a creep and watch me?"

"I think I can find a way to make this fun for both of us."

"What if"—she pauses, biting her lip—"what if I want to watch you too?"

"You need to come over when I'm back home. I want you in my hot tub."

"That sounds great," she agrees, setting the phone against the mirror so I can look at the entire tub, before turning on the water. "One of these days I want to move into a place that has a giant soaking tub."

"I've got that, too, Duchess."

She looks over her shoulder at the phone, after setting a couple towels on the ledge of the tub. "You're never beating the allegations that you just want me naked in your house."

"Couldn't deny it if I wanted." I watch her pull a basket off a shelf. "What are you looking for?"

"Trying to decide which bath bomb to use." Jess pulls out a pink foil ball. "This one makes great bubbles and smells like roses, but has me glittery for days." She puts it back and pulls out a purple one. "This one has lavender oil in it and helps me sleep, which could be good tonight. But this one"—she picks up one wrapped in black—"this one smells like you."

"Use that one. I want you to feel like I'm there with you."

CHAPTER 21
JESS

FRIENDS WITH BENEFITS are supposed to be kept quiet. Something secret. Just between us. Why, pray tell, does Valentin Fucking Bishop think it's a great idea to send me flowers and gifts to work while he's at an away game?

Lately, though, Bishop has been acting weird. Not in his usual "I'm a goalie" weird, which is to be expected and comes with his role, but he seems to almost be a boyfriend? What started off as a touching base for late night meet ups or dates at the club, has now turned into something a little more… domestic. It's not bad, if anything it feels comfortable, but I don't know if he is aware that he's doing it. The shift began with bringing hangover cures the morning after I called him over for a booty call when I had too many glasses of wine. He wouldn't touch me while I was drunk, and it was still mortifying to realize that I begged a man to come over to my house. He kept telling me no, but made sure I went to bed safely. Then he came over on a day where I went home sick, bringing me comfort foods and staying until I fell asleep. Booty calls do not bring you soup and make you grilled cheese, and they definitely don't snuggle or hold a heating pad to your screaming body. They also don't make sure you're safe and check on you the next morning.

The fact that I'm not running away that this giant, sometimes overbearing, ridiculous man might actually be entertaining. A relationship with him should scare me, but honestly the only thing really standing in our way is… us.

No, he doesn't want a real relationship. He has never ever in the history that I have known him, had one. That's why this works with us; no commitments, no strings, it's simple. I know this is what I signed up for, and I'm okay with that, but what if's are driving me crazy.

And now there's the gifts…

First, it was the lunch delivery. Granted it was well-timed because I hadn't ordered anything and it was already after two. I was trying to figure out if I could get away with living off of a soft pretzel from one of the concession stands before puck drop tonight at the charity alumni game. It was thoughtful, and just generic enough that I could blow it off as I forgot that I had ordered it earlier in the day.

But now there are flowers. I can't play them off as my own purchase, so I had to make up a boyfriend on the fly of course. This led to extra questioning from Ronni and Roby… and everyone else who walked past and noticed that my desk had been overtaken by a giant vase filled with reds and purples with a card that said it reminded him of my first drink we had together.

Who says that? Of all of the things to put on a card, a certain color of flower reminded him of a vodka cranberry?

The giftbox currently covering my keyboard is too big to shove in my drawer, which means it's going to be highly visible all day long and someone is going to start asking questions. Slowly, I untie the ribbon on top to see just what is inside this gold box. Tucked within the fluffy layers of tissue paper, with a brand tag that I could only dream of owning, sits the most beautiful black dress. Delicate straps, impeccable workmanship. My heart soars, thinking of how it will feel against me, and I smile imagining his face when I wear it.

Just as fast as I get the dopamine hit, I crash. What the hell are we doing? Booty calls don't buy dresses!

And the card?

I can see you in this with my favorite shoes. The way I want to see this on my bedroom floor. -V

Everything else had nothing showing where it came from. But this? With one of the most uncommon initials on the planet? If someone else sees this, we're so screwed.

Tucking the card away in my pocket, I grab my phone.

> Me: A dress? Really?

I watch three dots appear, disappear, and return.

> Bishop: Can't wait to see it Saturday night.

> Bishop: You're welcome, Duchess.

I sigh, willing my panic away.

> Me: Thank you, Sir.

> Me: But couldn't you have sent this to my house? Or yours?

The incoming call startles me, the phone landing with a soft rustle against the tissue paper. Of course he calls after this.

"It's beautiful, but…"

"You deserve beautiful things, Duchess. So, dinner Saturday?"

I chew on my lip nervously. "Your place or mine?"

"Neither. I have reservations for us at Nico's."

"Nico's? Where the team hangs out?"

"It's where they give us privacy. I don't want us to only ever sneak off to the club or our apartments."

"That sounds awfully 'date night' of you."

"Maybe. So, Saturday night? We're good?"

"Okay, just…" I sigh. "Enough with the work deliveries, people are starting to notice."

"Okay. I'll pick you up at seven, then."

"No, I'll meet you there. That way no one sees us arriving together."

Saying our goodbyes, I stare blankly at the box. I apparently have an actual date Saturday night.

Date night with Valentin Bishop. In public.

My heart swoops, and I can't decide if it's because I'm excited, nervous, or scared of what this means.

NICO'S IS a high-end restaurant that the players frequent that I've always heard of but have never visited. Standing at the bar, swirling my wine in the stemless glass, I wonder if it's too late to escape before he knows I'm here.

The dress he sent me fits like a glove, and paired with my shoes from the club, I love my look. I feel confident that I fit in with the crowd around me, but what will he think? Glancing down at my shoes, I notice a strap hanging loose.

"When did that happen?" I mutter, hopping up onto a barstool to see if I can reach down to fix it.

"Can I help you with that?" I pause, then glance up at a total stranger. "You look like you're struggling. I can get that for you if you'd like."

"Um… sure?" I look around, not seeing Bishop yet. Carefully, he kneels and gently grasps my ankle, holding with one hand sliding the loose strap back into the buckle. "Thank you."

"Anytime, it would be a tragedy if you fell."

"That's sweet. I'm–"

"Getting into trouble without me, Duchess?" At hearing his voice, I stop breathing. Looking away from the helpful stranger, I find Bishop standing less than a foot from me, an indulgent smile on his face. "I've got it from here, kid. Thanks."

"Sorry, of course. I'll get out of your way," he says, popping up to stand, holding a hand out. "Truly enjoy watching you play with the Ice Wolves."

Bishop stares down at the man's hand, then back at my ankle, up to my face, and back to him. Grasping his hand firmly, he flashes his camera-ready smile I'm all too familiar with, responding, "Thanks. And thank you for taking care of my girl."

His girl?

"An honor, truly. Wouldn't want her to get hurt."

"Certainly. Have a good night." Bishop's tone leaves no room for continuing the conversation, and in catching the hidden meeting, the man walks off.

"Wow, why don't you just mark your territory next time?" I chirp, smirking up at the stony face of my date.

"It's messy and not my preferred kink." I snort at his dry, factual delivery. "Let me see your shoe, Duchess."

Without breaking eye contact, I slide my ankle up the side of his leg, until his large hand wraps around my ankle—an echo of the move a few moments ago. With gentle touches, he tugs on the individual straps, making sure they're firm before motioning for me to give him my other foot. I swap letting him check the other. Satisfied with his findings, he lets go, then steps close enough to me that I have to crane my neck to see his face.

"Nico, can I get my usual, please? We're heading to the private dining room now. Thanks," he calls over my head to the man behind the bar, then leans in and murmurs beside my ear, "Come on, before you have the rest of the bar kneeling at your feet." He takes my wineglass in one hand while holding his other out for me to balance with.

Sliding off the barstool, I let myself into his personal

space, feeling his hard muscle against me. "Thank you, Sir," I whisper, knowing what that will do to him. I hear his breath catch before I walk away.

"Sneaky brat," he chuckles, sliding a hand around my hip as he guides me to the private dining in the back. "Have I told you how beautiful you look tonight?"

"Oh, you like this look?" I gesture to my dress as holds the door open for me, his hungry eyes locked on mine.

"Love it, I should buy you pretty things more often," he comments, closing the door behind him. "Although maybe I shouldn't let you out of my sight."

"Getting rather possessive, aren't you?" I tease a little too breathlessly, circling one of the high-top tables to face him. He prowls the short distance toward me, like a predator stalking his prey, then sets the wineglass on the table, unrushed. It's as if he knows I'm exactly where he wants me, no rush to chase me. I lick my lips, waiting anxiously for him to come closer.

"I don't need to be possessive. You're mine, Duchess." The phrase is factual but neutral, and I like it a bit too much.

AFTER A NIGHT of drinks and essentially dry humping on the dance floor, curling up on my couch with my Duchess feels oddly domesticated, but also completely right. Her calves resting across my thighs, my hands rub up and down her smooth skin, massaging her ankles on the down stroke, and then repeating the motion up the length of her legs, over and over. It's soothing, which is a hell of a lot more than I can say about the email I just received from my club manager tonight, with lower than normal door counts. With a frustrated sigh, I take my hand off of her ankle so I can type effectively.

She pauses, sitting up at my shifted mood, with her forehead wrinkled in confusion. "Are you okay?"

"Yeah, I will be. Door counts are down at the club."

"What promotions are you running at the moment? Where have you put your ad revenue?"

I look up from my screen, tilting my head and confusion at her, surprised she's interested in my business. "We don't really promote, because it's a private club, but membership numbers have been down lately."

"That's what I'm talking about: what are you doing to

improve numbers? Have you done any sort of event to draw new members in? And why are members staying away? Are they withdrawing membership, or are they just not visiting as frequently?" She continues, and while I can see her plush lips moving, the words coming out of her mouth don't compute. "Bishop." My name brings me back to reality. "Who is doing your PR work? Do you have any marketing at all? Who on your team is responsible for all of this?"

"Well… I don't really have one," I offer, a little confused by her line of questioning and how it relates to load door counts.

"Oh my God, how are you supposed to run a business if you don't have anybody marketing for you?" She sits up straighter, starting to move her legs off of mine, before I latch a hand on her ankle. "If you don't have someone on your social media and marketing, how do you expect anyone to know that the club even exists? Hell, the only reason I found you that night was because I stumbled into the VIP section on accident, because it wasn't marked. Is the front of the house getting decent door counts?"

"It's pretty steady, enough to stay in the black."

"Staying in the black is hardly a successful business model," she drawls, rolling her eyes. "Have you tried having themed nights, where you have kink educators come in to discuss techniques? Shibari demonstrations?"

"No," I shake my head, thinking it over. "Would people actually come to that?"

"Are you serious right now?" She grabs her phone, taps the screen a few times, then flips her search screen so I can read it. Dozens of hits from other clubs with exactly that theme fill her screen. "What are the demographics of the membership list? Have you done anything to bring in women? To make LGBTQ members comfortable? Or did you just set up a club and think it would run itself and be self-sufficient?"

"Well… kinda," I respond, my tone a little defensive.

"You need to have a reason for everyone to want to come back or to have a reason to come in the first place. Especially if your demographics are skewed and there's maybe one female client up for hetero activities for every five hetero guys that are in there? It's no wonder Chad latched onto me as soon as he spotted me," she snarks, opening up a fresh document on her phone. "And you have nobody running your marketing?"

"I could hire you." She shoots me a dark look, and I almost consider walking the statement back.

I never walk statements back. What the hell.

"Absolutely not. It's bad enough we're already doing this and HR would have a field day if they do. I absolutely refuse to fuck you while working directly underneath you, at the same time."

"Okay, fine. Not officially working for me, but what would you do if you did? How would you fix this?"

"You want free marketing lessons?"

"You're the expert."

She eyes me suspiciously, then concedes, "First, I would need to look at the membership statistics over the last year. When is everybody coming? Why are they stopping or slowing their attendance? What are the demographics that we're working with? Where are your weak spots? And then there's your promo… The only way to get people in the door is to give them a reason to come in said door. You did a solid job, making sure I was comfortable in that space, but what about other female clientele? Are they comfortable coming in? Do they have a reason to feel safe or is there a reason for them to want to? Or is the whole place being a sausage party of guys looking for girls keeping the ladies away? From the times I visited, how open is the space for LGBTQ, non-binary, polyam… how many other groups are welcomed in, or do they feel left out?" I just stare at her as she goes on and on, asking questions, taking mental notes asI let her voice roll over me. "Bishop, are you even listening to me?"

"Yeah, you asked questions," I reply, knowing that my answer does not even encompass the whole thing. "A lot of them. I got distracted because you have no idea how hot you are when you start talking business."

"And this is the exact reason that I can't work underneath you."

"Pity," I murmur, caressing her ankle again. "It would be so much fun if you did."

"You would be even less useful than you are currently," she chirps back. "I should go home soon, you have morning practice."

"Or you could spend the night and we could carpool. Save gas. Good for the environment."

"Friends with benefits don't spend the night, Bishop," she quips, swinging her feet to the floor. "See you on the ice tomorrow."

Jess leans over to kiss me softly before walking away. I sigh to myself rubbing at the ache in my chest as the door clicks shut. I need her a hell of a lot more than she needs me.

NOTHING CURES a girl's problems like emergency brunch. It's why I'm sitting at my favorite cafe away from the rink, waiting on Ronni. I need my best girl friend's input after whatever that was with Bishop.

I can't tell Robicheaux, he'll either freak out or spill his guts to Kozlov, who will say something to Bishop. That won't help matters. He's too close to be objective. Ronni will be able to be reasonable.

I watch the door for her, glancing nervously at my phone for the time. Swiping open our text thread, I pause, feeling eyes on me. I glance up again, to see if she's here, except she's not. I continue scrolling my phone for a few minutes, clicking on a few emails to mark them important, when Ronni's sweet voice calls, "I'm so glad you asked me out!" breaking me out of my spiraling thoughts.

"Me too, girl, I needed this!" I reply, tucking my phone away and standing up to hug her in greeting. "I already put in our usual order."

"Oh thank heavens; I'm starving! And the mimosas are already here!"

Ronni's excitement is infectious, and I can't help but smile back. We drop into our seats, clink glasses, and settle into a comfortable silence as we sip the sweet drink.

"So," I start, pulling a few more strawberries onto my plate, "I need to ask you something. I need some help."

"Anything! What's going on?"

"You absolutely cannot tell Moxley about this. Okay? It stays here."

"What happens at brunch, stays at brunch. It's girl code." She places a hand across her heart, looking at me solemnly. "As long as you're okay… and safe."

"Oh, yeah, definitely safe," I confirm. "I, well… I might be seeing someone."

"Good for you," she praises, picking up her champagne flute. "And about damn time! So, tell me all about him. Is he hot? Does he treat you well? Is that the guy who was sending you flowers and gifts?"

"He does treat me well, and that's the problem, I think." I pause sipping my drink. "We aren't supposed to be in a relationship."

"What do you mean? How do you end up in a relationship if you aren't supposed to… Oh." Her eyes widen. "Was this the guy from the club a while back?"

"Yeah, it's him. I think he's attached. He's being very boyfriend-coded."

"He has really good taste. Those flowers were gorgeous." She nods in agreement. "Where's the drawback? Does he smell like onions? Is he bad at sex?" She gasps. "Oh no, is he married?"

"No, nothing like that. He's just slightly off-limits."

"You said he wasn't married, the only way he could be off limits would be… Oh, shit, is he a player?"

I close my eyes, afraid to see her reaction when I admit the truth. "Yeah, he is."

"Oh, wow, so it is true." I look up at her and surprise, tilt my head. Why is she not surprised about this? "I thought Mox was just trying to play a trick on me."

"What does Moxley know?"

"He swore me to secrecy, and I honestly didn't believe him when he told me. But apparently your guy was asking for help on the plane to the away game a couple weeks ago, and may have mentioned you by name."

I'm going to kill that gorgeous goalie the next time I see him. "He told Moxley? He's the worst with secrets—worse than Robicheaux is—and I didn't tell him for that exact reason!"

"In his defense, I don't think he knew how to process it, and he was also kind of worried about how"—she glances around to ensure no one is within earshot—"*you know who* was treating you. They may be close friends, but he knows you're my closest friend, so he wanted to make sure he wasn't blind to any issues."

I sigh in relief; she seems to be taking it well. "So you're not mad at me?"

"As long as you're happy, and I don't have to send my boyfriend to go beat him up, then we'll be good to go."

"Yeah, we don't need to go beating up anyone ," I laugh. "Part of the problem is he does treat me well, and I think I could see us being in a solid relationship, but that's not what we started with. I don't know if we can at this point. I mean, what do I even know about him that isn't already in a press release?"

"Well, you know more about him than most people. He's notoriously private, and if he's let you in even the slightest bit, that has to say something."

She has a point, I've learned more about him in the few months since we met at the club than I have in all of my time working next to the press. "Is that enough? And not to mention the same thing that you ran into with Moxley. We're from two different worlds, and professionally it's going to cause a problem."

"But will it, really? I know I worried about it with El because anything could happen. And they still kept me on. Now look at us."

Her positivity, while reassuring, doesn't totally relieve me. Just because the Ice Wolves did it once, doesn't mean they'll do it again. "Maybe I'll give him a shot, but I should keep an eye out for another job, just in case things do go sideways. I don't really want to leave, but we'll cross that bridge when we get there."

"*If* you get there. Maybe they'll move you into my office and we can work side by side again! I miss having you around all day," she pouts.

"I know what you mean, I–" I freeze, looking around.

"Are you okay?"

"Yeah, I just felt strange for a second. You know when it feels like someone's watching you but you don't know who or where? It feels like that."

"You're just paranoid because you're sneaking around with a hot goalie." She clinks her glass to mine. "Take a minute to relax, you've earned it."

CHAPTER 25
BISHOP

COMING HOME from an away game always feels good. Knowing that I'm coming home and can see Jess, though, this is new. Exciting. I can't remember the last time I looked forward to something like this.

Opening my apartment door, I expect to be greeted by dead silence. Instead, I hear pop music coming from my kitchen.

"Viv?" I call out. "Don't you have your own kitchen?"

"Yeah, but yours has the really good coffee in it!" I step into the dining room, finding my sister pouring a fresh cup. "Want one?"

"No, I'm heading back out. I just stopped by to drop off my bag and change."

"Ah," she responds knowingly. "You're headed to Jess's."

"How do you know–"

"I'm your twin, duh. We just know things. And besides, you left your phone unlocked the other day."

"That doesn't give you permission to go through it," I grumble.

"Anyway," she continues, as if I didn't accuse her of invading my privacy. "You're heading over to her place?"

"Maybe. Or seeing if she wants to go out."

"With no warning? Baby bro, that's not going to work."

"But how else am I supposed to see her?"

"You send her a text and see what she's doing," she huffs. "You don't show up on her doorstep like some weirdo!"

"I already sent a text, she didn't answer yet. I'm just going to take her dinner or something. Knowing her, she's elbows-deep in work and forgot what time it was."

Viv's eyes light up, and she points at me accusingly. "You like her, don't you? Like, not just a booty call 'like' her…"

"How are we only five minutes apart?" I tut, leaving the room. "I'm out of here, make sure you shut the coffee maker off before you leave."

"Make wise choices!" She yells at my back, her cackle echoing in the kitchen.

SCANNING across the club at the crowd that's formed, I can't deny the dozens of butterflies that have taken in my stomach. Bishop actually listened to me, and here we stand at his first ever Shibari course at the club. Pride blooms in my chest. He hired a reputable educator to come in and demonstrate safe practices, all because I recommended it.

The members murmur excitedly around me as we wait for it to start. Bishop's backstage, but said he'd be right out once he confirmed a few things. My fingers twist nervously around the stem of the wine flute in front of me. I really wish I'd requested a stemless glass to avoid my fidgeting.

"Enjoying yourself, Duchess?" Bishop purrs from behind me, dropping a kiss just under my ear. The shiver of excitement runs down my spine and I hum in response.

"Are they ready to go?"

"They are," he replies quietly, taking a seat on the stool beside me.

One of the managers, acting as MC of the event, steps onto the stage platform, and the crowd around us hushes in anticipation. After welcoming everyone and introducing the guest speaker, the presentation begins, and Bishop and I settle in.

The instructor is gentle, explaining different examples of rigging and materials that can be safely used. While demonstrating ties on their partner, I feel Bishop lean in close, his heat enveloping me.

"Getting ideas?" His words are soft, barely more than a whisper against the shell of my ear, but they hit me everywhere. Hell, I shouldn't be surprised, this man could dismantle me without a single word.

I nod, never taking my eyes off the pair before us. The instructor and their partner are both beautiful, and I'm enthralled. The partner chimes in with education from their point of view being tied up. Looking out at the room, everyone's eyes are on them, enjoying the workshop, but there's one person, off in a corner, staring back at me. I can't make out features from this distance and in the dim light, but it makes me feel extremely uncomfortable. A shiver creeps down my spine, and I try to shake off the gross interaction.

"You okay, Duchess?" Bishop whispers, holding me close.

"Yeah, I just saw someone I thought... Nevermind."

While I'm trying to pay attention, I can't shake the feeling that we're being watched more than the Shibari instructor. As the demonstration wraps up, I muster the courage to find the person again, and find the corner empty.

"Want to go to the room and play?"

His question brings me back to the present, shaking away what must've been a random patron watching the demonstration and not me. "Yes, Sir." I feel his groan vibrate through my back as he pulls me close, kissing my neck again.

"Let's say goodbye to our guests first."

"Our guests?"

He doesn't reply as he takes my hand, walking us up to the edge of the stage where the demonstrators are answering questions about the display pieces. He shakes their hands, and retrieves a hemp rope before pulling me away.

THE BUZZ of a tattoo needle greets me as I walk into the studio. Jess thought I wouldn't do it, that I wasn't serious? Joke's on her, really, because here I am, and I know just the thing to do.

I give her five minutes to see the notification on her phone where I texted her the address. Knowing my girl, she'll be here in under an hour, and by then, the deed will be done. She'll be etched into my skin like she is on my soul.

My phone chirps in my pocket, and I grin as I see the text thread.

Me: 907 N. 15th St.

Duchess: What's that?

Me: Come find me.

Duchess: Okay...?

Duchess: Give me a minute.

I grin, she has no idea what this is, and I'm sure she'll be pissed about it for a minute, but she's worth it.

"Bishop! Long time no see, man!" My favorite artist makes his way across the room, wiping his hands dry on a paper towel. "I have your stencil over here if you're ready."

I look over the delicate script spelling Duchess, that will go right at my collarbone, visible over my jersey. It's beautiful, just like she is.

"It's perfect, Sid. Let's do it."

I strip my t-shirt, and stand still as he places the stencil carefully. As I settle on the patted table, my gut churns a little. What if I'm wrong? What if she actually hates it?

Tough. It's mine. She's mine. And if I want to brand her on me where everyone can see it, I will.

The vibrations reverberate through me, and paired with the scratching of the needle across my skin, I revel in the feel of it. Tattoo therapy may not be a clinically approved thing, but damn, if it doesn't help. I close my eyes and relax, letting Sid work his magic like he always has.

"Val, why did you summon me to– Is that a tattoo?" Jess's voice carries to me like a siren call from the front of the shop. I take a break as Sid wipes at my skin to roll my head slowly in her direction.

"Hey, Duchess. About time you made it."

"What the hell are you doing? You're getting– Is that my *name*? You can't be serious right now."

"Of course I am," I reply matter of factly, as if it was the simplest thing on Earth. "I'm yours. How else could I show you?"

"There are so many ways, but a tattoo? That's so... permanent!"

"Typically, yes."

"And it's going to be visible in all of your shoots! I can't photoshop every photo!"

"Not really concerned about what the team thinks right now."

"But it's *permanent*," she repeats, softer.

"I know, I mean this. Come here, I want to see you."

She floats into my space, taking my upturned hand in hers. Her eyes are wide locked on my throat. I swallow reflexively under gaze, and I'm barely aware of Sid nudging me.

"Sit still, man, I'm almost done," he laughs before turning to Jess. "Would you like a seat? You can hang out while I finish, if you'd like."

Wordlessly, his apprentice brings in a chair, and offers her a drink. She sits, never letting go of my hand.

"On a scale of one to cutting my balls off, how pissed are you?" I hedge.

She shoots me a look that should be intimidating, but just makes me smile stupidly at her. She can't stay mad, clearly, and she smiles back. "It's kind of sweet, but you could've told me about it first."

"What's the fun in that? Besides, this one is for me. I have another one that's for you."

Her eyebrows furrow in confusion. "What are you talking about?"

"Are we doing it? You're going for the knuckles?"

"If she says yes, then we absolutely are."

"I'm not saying yes until I know what it is," she says, her eyes narrowing in suspicion. "What tattoo is mine if it isn't my name on your chest?"

"Exactly," I respond cryptically.

"That isn't really an answer."

"Sid, you have the stencils ready?"

"Yeah, let me just wrap this first."

Once he's finished, he cleans up the new tattoo with broad strokes of the towel before placing the clear wrapping over top. Satisfied, he gets up, walks over to a counter, and brings over a sheet with four distinct letters on them. I sit up, but watch her face closely behind me. Of all the decisions taken out of my hands, this one feels like the biggest at the moment.

"M...I...N...E..." she pauses. "Mine? On your knuckles? Why?"

I slip off the seat and walk behind her. "So when I do this..." I slide my hand along the hinge of her jaw, turning so we can both look in the mirror together. "You can see what's mine, as much as I'm yours." Her breath catches as I squeeze gently on the sides of her throat, but she melts against me, and I grin in victory as her eyelashes flutter shut. "You like that, don't you? Want me to claim you every chance I get?" It's a statement, not a question; I know my girl too well.

"Yeah, I do." Her answer is barely a breath, and my heart swells, victorious.

A HOME GAME after a week on the road feels amazing. The crowd energy is electric, and the feedback to our play reminds us of why we do this. I spot Jess nearby, Ronni by her side, looking on proudly. They're both wearing jerseys, Ronni's with a "C" on the front, wearing Moxley's number. He's going to be insufferable when he sees it. I try to glance at the sleeves to make out the number on Jess's jersey but I can't tell. She would be sexy as hell in mine. Maybe I can sweet talk her into one some night, or convince her to wear it with nothing on underneath while at my place.

Focus, Bishop. You have a game to play.

The third period just started, and I'm feeling pretty good about keeping this 3-0 score, but I don't dare lose focus now. Moxley and Robicheaux are at the opposite end of the ice, giving the Las Vegas Generals goalie some hell with their game of keepaway. I zero in on the puck—left to Roby, right to Mox, dumped back to Kozlov, back to Mox. Their defense is wearing down, chasing them.

"Come on, boys, keep it up," I mutter in my mask. A flurry of activity happens, and the direction of play changes. A General player knocks away the puck, kicking it back into the neutral zone and onto the stick of their center. "Oh, here we go." My heart races, the excitement of play locking me in. Roby catches up faster than Mox, jockeying with our opponent for control of the puck.

A Generals player checks Moxley, knocking his stick out of his hands, whipping it across to Roby, catching Roby's blade. Roby superman-dives onto the ice in front of me, flying head-first toward the pipe. The General player he's been battling is right on top of him.

I have less than a second to figure out who's going into the pipe. Roby or me.

I dive in front of them, catching Roby with my blocker.

Fuck, that's gonna hurt.

———

The rank smell of hospital is the first thing I notice as I try to pry my heavy eyelids open.

Dark hair covers my forearm, and I rasp out, "Duchess?" My fuzzy brain struggles to make sense of what I'm seeing, and at my word, she lifts her head.

"Holy shit, you're awake." She reaches over for a cup of water on the tray table beside her. "Here, drink this." She holds out a plastic cup with a tiny straw. "You scared us last night."

"Us?" The cool water is a relief and all too soon she's taking it away from me.

"Me. You scared me last night."

"What happened?"

"What do you remember?"

"Breakaway, bad check, Roby… Is Roby okay?"

"You broke his fall, probably saved him going on concussion protocol, but they're watching you instead. Replay looks like you lost consciousness for a bit. They've had you on a concoction of things since you were admitted."

"Feels like I got hit by a bus." I let my eyes drift close again, and try to do a physical check. Toes wiggle, ankles roll, knees feel normal, hips... "Shit, that hurts."

"They both landed on you. Roby and that rookie on the Generals."

I crack my eyes open again, looking down at my hands. Fingers attached, no slings, just an IV on one side, and my Duchess on the other. "How long am I out?"

"Don't know. They aren't telling me much. Viv knows more, since she's family."

"Where is she?"

"Woody took her back to the arena to get your car and stuff from your locker. She'll be back soon."

"Good kid," I murmur, feeling sleep try to drag me down again. "So tired."

"Oh good, you're awake," a familiar woman's voice from the door breaks into my near slip into unconsciousness. My mind is fuzzy and it takes way longer than it should to place who it is.

I only get a brief look at her, then croak, "Viv, you're loud," eyes slamming shut against the overstimulation.

"Yeah, yeah, and you've been practically dead for the last four hours."

"Hey Bishop," Woody calls, his voice soft. "Glad to see you up again."

I feel Jess slip her hands off of mine, leaving me cold and ungrounded. "I wouldn't say 'up,' yet," I respond. "Did you end up..."

"Off the bench? Yeah."

"He saved the shutout you started," Viv interjects.

"Good job, rook."

"You had it most of the way there." He waves off the praise. "Seemed like a waste to let it get that far and lose it. Coach already told me to hold down your spot for the next few games."

"You've got this, kid. I have all the faith in you."

"I should go, we just didn't want you to wake up alone," Jess says, moving to get up.

"No, stay," Viv protests. "You're good for him."

I watch Jess' eyes dart between me, Viv, and Woody—who is standing in the corner like an awkward statue. "He won't say anything," I assure her.

"Okay," she whispers, sliding her hand back into mine.

Fighting off the heaviness of my eyes feels like too much, as I let myself drift off.

———

As I feel myself floating at the edge of consciousness, I enjoy the smell of Jess's shampoo, loving her warmth against my side. I could stay like this forever.

"Bish, buddy, are you– J-lo? What the hell are you doing here?" Robicheaux's voice jars me back into the current state. The throbbing ache in my head doubles as Jess's comfort is ripped away from me.

"Robes, it's not what it looks like. I mean, maybe it is, but I can explain," she babbles, the chair screeching across the tiles as she shifts farther away from me.

"It looks like you were snuggling my goalie. What's the deal?"

"Roby, too loud," I mutter, trying to open my eyes.

"Hey, shh, go back to sleep, I'll take him out of here," Jess whispers, running her fingertips along my arm lightly. "I'll be right back." As she moves away, her tone cools, "Come on, we're talking in the hall."

I feel my face lift into a smile. She's going to eat him alive out there, and I love it.

ANGER THRUMS in my chest as I walk ahead of my friend, trying to rehearse what I'm going to tell him.

"Jess, talk to me, what are you doing? I don't understand–"

"Not here," I bite out, grabbing a fistful of his sweatshirt and pulling us into the stairwell, taking the steps two at a time.

"We could have taken the elevator."

"No, because it stops too often, and someone will get in. I need the silence."

"I mean, we could have stayed in his room, then."

"No, he needs his rest. He's had a long damn night and this isn't helping." I can hear my voice growing shrill and echoing off the brick but I can't stop as I stand on a landing. "I've been here all night with him and he gets woken up every half hour for tests and rounds and his sister coming in, and he needs rest and—"

"Hey," he shushes, coming down to my level and pulling me into his arms. "I get it, I do, I'm just surprised that you're here with him, okay?"

My sanity cracks, and I sob into my best friend's shoulder. "I'm sorry, I should've–"

"Wait… are you his mystery girl?"

"What?" I pull back to look at him closer.

"His mystery girl. The guys have been giving him shit about some girl he's wrapped up with. Trying to buy her gifts to impress her. Oh my God!" His eyes go wide. "He was… you were… that was…"

"Words, Robes. I don't follow."

"The night at the club. You met a guy."

"Yeah, I did. I never said who."

"And then your vanilla date, he went…" Roby stares, blank faced as his thoughts whir through his skull. It's like I can see images flash in his head. "He disappeared after that."

"Wait. Huh?"

"Okay. Okay, okay, okay," he mutters, breathing deeply. "Let's get some coffee and talk because I think my mind is blown. And you two have some explaining to do!" He looks at my tearstained face, wiping gently at the tracks. "I'm not mad, I'm just surprised. Okay?"

I nod, shakily. This could have gone way worse. I take the stairs slower, Roby at my back. We make our way to the cafeteria for coffee, and with drink in hand, I offer, "We should take these back to his room, so he's not alone."

"Nah, he'll be okay. We should talk without him first. There's a spot in the atrium that's quiet," he answers, approaching the coffee cart and ordering our drinks as I float nearby.

Gathering our steaming cups, he motions me toward the glass enclosed space, pointing out a bench tucked in a corner between some greenery. The sunlight feels nice, and the sense of privacy behind the statuary is a nice change from the claustrophobic enclosure of the room upstairs.

"I'm sorry I didn't tell you sooner," I add, holding my cup

in both hands and letting the warmth seep into my numb fingers. "I don't know where to start."

"The beginning might be good," he says softly, letting one arm rest on the back of the bench as he shifts to face me.

"It might get awkward," I warn, shifting to face him in return.

"J, babe, you've fielded social media comments asking if Koz and I are together-together, in specific detail. I don't know if there's much between us that can make us uncomfortable."

He's right, I think, nodding. "Okay, so the night at the club." I pause making sure he's following. "Bishop was the one who scared off the guy who wouldn't leave me alone."

"That sounds like him."

"We didn't exchange names or anything. I didn't know it was him. He was just really nice, and we talked, and kind of hit it off. So, we," I bite my lip, thinking of how to go on. "We went to his room."

He nods knowingly. "You can spare me the details there. I know what the room is about."

"I saw the tattoo and ran afterward, because I was scared. And then there was the conference room. I delivered a presentation to some of the trustees and Bishop was there, and he figured out I was the girl from the club. Apparently, he had been trying to figure out who she was. Anyway, I panicked because we can't talk like that at work, you know?"

"That's fair. I know Ronni and Mox had the same issues."

"So, that was before that vanilla date. And after he crashed that, we talked about being just," I cringe, "friends with benefits? No strings attached. Nothing serious."

"You looked awfully serious in his room just now. When did things change?"

"I can't even pinpoint it. But I think... No. I know. We can't go back to that."

"You're attached."

"We both are, honestly. But we still can't tell anyone, because he's him and I'm, well, me."

"Have you talked to Ronni? She just went through something similar and might have some advice."

"Yeah, and apparently Moxley's been trying to help Bishop figure out his side, too, but it's still not a great situation to be in. And, seriously, what does this look like, with two members of the team hooking up with PR at almost the same time? The office isn't a dating agency."

"No, it's not," he agrees, "but you also can't help who you fall for. So you two have been dating on the side?"

"I don't know if dating is the right word for it, but we have been spending a lot of time together. He's really a good guy, under all the quiet and grumpy exterior."

"If anyone on the team was going to steal you, I'm glad it's him."

"He's not stealing anything, Robes. I'm still my own person." I frown. "I'm not a possession."

"I know. But I also get the feeling that you're going to want for nothing with this one around."

"He is kind of hyperfocused," I say with a watery laugh. "He does make me happy."

"Good. You should be with someone that puts your happiness first. Hallmark movies say so."

"I thought they said to move to a small town from the big city and save a Christmas tree farm," I joke.

"If that's what brings you happiness, yes. Now, should we go back up and see your man?"

"Yeah, let's go. But, Roby? Can we keep this between us, maybe just you and Koz? I don't want things to get weird with the team."

"You got it."

I SHOULD HAVE WARNED Jess that I'm a royal terror when I'm benched for an injury. Viv knows, and has been running interference between my growly ass and Jess's attempts to take care of me. I have too much built up energy and not enough activity or range of motion to do anything about it.

For the fifth day in a row, I'm camped out on my living room couch watching game recaps, and regretting diving to save Robicheaux. I wouldn't want him hurt, I would have felt like shit watching a friend and teammate crack into the pipes, too. A selfish part of me knows that if he did, he'd be the one sitting on the couch with nothing to do, instead of me. I heave a sigh of irritation as I watch a puck slip past Woody last night on a screen play.

"He fell for that backhand again," I grumble as my young backup clears the net for the ref as the Gators celebrate behind him.

"He's still young, you know that," Viv counters, settling on the couch beside me with two steaming cups of tea. "Here, drink something. The lack of caffeine the last few days has turned you into a beast."

I glance sideways at her, ignoring the pain in my head. Concussion protocol as a precaution, they said. No screens, no rink time, and no caffeine. Just rest. As if I could. "I'm not a beast," I grumble, taking the cup and sniffing it cautiously. "What is this?"

"Green tea, with lemon. Not enough caffeine to mess with you but maybe enough to get you to stop being bitchy."

"Fuck off," I grumble, taking a sip anyway. It's nice, soothing, and it gives me something to do with my hands. "I'm not trying to be a dick, I'm just…"

"You're bored and you don't like sitting around. I know. It's like I've been here before," she says, sarcastically, rolling her eyes. "But Jess hasn't and you need to be careful with that one. Don't scare her off, I like her."

"I'm trying," I grumble, sipping more tea. "I just feel helpless."

"So tell her that. Communicate. You're not flying solo here."

"I know," I start, "it's just that I'm not meant for…" I wave a hand in the general direction of the brace and ice packs.

"We know that, just relax and let someone take care of you for once in your sorry life," she says, looking past my head, before hissing softly, "She's bringing you a snack, you'd better be grateful."

I look over at Jess, bringing me a plate with some of Woody's protein cookies. "I thought you might want some of these, he brought them over yesterday before the game." She sits down beside me, placing the plate in my lap where my one good hand can reach them, before settling down beside me., *I could get used to this.*

We watch a Gator player sink another puck behind Woody's blind spot. "God damn it, I taught him better than that!" I roar, frustration taking over. The action startles Jess, who bumps the plate, causing a small avalanche of crumbs across the couch.

"And you all say we're the overly emotional gender," she mutters, picking up the remnants of cookies from around us. "Lucky I love you or I'd have left you on your own by now," she mutters under her breath as she sets everything back to where it should be.

I freeze. Replaying the last few moments in the living room, ignoring the mess on the screen. "You… love me?" I whisper the words, not fully believing them myself. Her eyes go wide, locking on mine. "Say it again."

"What?"

"What did you just say? Say it again. Please."

"I don't know…" I raise an eyebrow at her, and she sighs in response. "Okay, fine. I said… you're lucky I love you."

My face aches from smiling at her, and her mock anger melts into a smile of her own. "I love you too."

LIFE IS GOOD. Bishop and I have come to an understanding of what our relationship consists of, and we had one of the most amazing weekends together. Record numbers spiked at the club after the demonstration like I told him it would, and our friends all seem to be on board with us being a "Thing" with a capital T.

I gather up my phone and camera from my desk, and make my way toward the locker rooms. One more home game on the books, then we're on winter break. Bishop is talking about taking me to this cabin he has for a getaway, and I cannot wait.

"Jess, can I see you in my office for a minute?" Michael calls from the doorway.

"Sure thing, be right there," I respond, sitting down the camera to come back before it later. He seems distracted, but this job has done nothing but stress him out for the last few years. I gather my meeting notebook and pen, just in case, and head to his corner office.

I always expect to see him sitting behind his desk. What I don't ever expect to see is the head of HR sitting opposite of him. They give cordial greetings and sit in the extra empty chair across from his desk, waiting for one of them to speak

"Jessica, I'm sure you are curious why we are gathered here right now," a sour looking HR manager starts. It's at this moment that I noticed the file folder in their hand—with my name on it.

"I am curious, I haven't heard anything about reorganization." Stay calm, I tell myself, and I force my corporate smile firmly onto my face.

"We received some disturbing news about your activities outside of work. As I'm sure you're aware, the Rockville Ice Wolves have a strong anti-fraternization policy in place, and it was present when you signed your employment on-boarding paperwork."

What the hell?

I try to figure out what they might be... And then it hits me. After work activities. Anti-fraternization. They found out about Bishop.

"We received information that you have been entertaining a member of the roster, and that is in direct violation of this policy as distasteful as this is, I feel like you need to see this."

A handful of photographs are laid on the edge of Michael's desk, face down in between us. I shoot a look at Michael, who is working extra hard not to make eye contact with me. He knows what these photos contain. I gather them off the glossy surface and carefully face the images. The stills are clearly from within the club, from the other night while Bishop and I admired the selection of restraints in one shot, he's holding fur-lined cuffs to my wrists as I gaze into his face, with an excited smile in my face. In another, I have my hand wrapped around his tie, pulling him close for a kiss. Another has me sitting on Bishop's lap, his fingertips just under the edge of the hem of my dress, and I flush as I remember what happened exactly two seconds later.

We are so busted.

"Am I allowed to ask where you may have acquired these photos?" I try my damnedest to keep my voice steady, but I want to know.

"A concerned citizen sent them over earlier this week, and after further investigation, we have reason to believe that these were not fabricated. Do you have anything to say for yourself?"

My chest aches as my heart beats wildly and panic, angry that our privacy had been violated, fear that this would affect not just my employment, but Bishop's as well with his injury. I knew this was a possibility, I knew this could happen. I told Bishop if this ever got out, I would be the one on the chopping block, and I was right.

"I don't know what to say," I reply hoarsely.

"Is this true?" Michael asks softly.

I don't trust my voice to answer, so I simply nod my head. He closes his eyes, sighs in disappointment as his head bows over his desk. "I'm sorry," I whisper.

"First Veronica, and now you?"

"You know, Michael, I might have a reason to be concerned about your leadership if this is a patterned event. Are you allowing your staff to fraternize with the players?"

"Michael had nothing to do with any of this, he didn't know." I practically spit the words at the toad sitting beside me.

"You covered for Ms. Snow, and now this?"

"He didn't cover for anybody, he wasn't involved!" Panic builds in my chest as I sit and help mostly watch Michael get a dressing down in front of me for something he had no idea took place "If you're here to fire me, can we just get it over with? Michael is innocent. If you're coming for my job because I fell in love with a goalie, then so be it. Show me where to sign."

GAME PREPARATION IS A SCIENCE. Routine, order, it's a calming presence in the midst of chaos. I should have known that something was up when the order and routine was anything but. Being greeted in the hallway, not by my woman, but instead by a couple of random interns, should've been my first clue—she didn't say anything about not getting to do the tunnel today. Now there's Ronni and Moxley in the hallway, not sucking each other's faces off, having an intense conversation in hushed whispers. Fighting before a game is always a bad move, he knows that.

"Trying to throw him off his game?" I toss at Ronni, hoping I could break the tension.

"Bishop, you haven't seen Jess today, have you?"

"No, I thought she was going to be doing the tunnel, but it's a couple of stupid interns down there," I reply. Even though they know about our relationship, I'm not about to tell them that I just saw her this morning before she left my apartment.

"El, will you fill him in? I'm going to see if she went back to her apartment, since I don't really have to be here for another couple hours."

"Here, take my keys. Tell her it will all work out in the end, okay?" She kisses him on the cheek, taking the ring of keys from his offered hand, and walks back the direction that I just came from.

"What is she talking about, Mox?"

Elliot frowns as if I should already know. "Jess was let go today, because you guys got outed."

"What?"

"Someone had pictures of you two together, and sent them upstairs."

"Fuck I've gotta go," I rush out. "This is my fucking fault."

"We've got a game in three hours," he reminds. I try calling Jess, but she doesn't pick up. "Keep calling, she's got to answer eventually."

"Fuck the game." We both freeze, because that is a statement that I have never in my life ever uttered. The game has always come first.

"Chicken." He blurts out the word. I can't figure out why he would say that.

"What?"

"Tell the trainers you got bad chicken. I'll cover for you." I take a deep breath, trying to calm my racing emotions. "They've got to give a reason for you leaving, and not dressing for the game. Food poisoning is the best I've got for you. Coach won't say much after the Norovirus game last year where half the team puked at the bench."

"Yeah, okay, you're right. I'll tell them I got sick and I'm in no shape to dress for the game."

I head to Coach's office, loosening my tie as I go. I spew some bullshit about bad chicken and not wanting to puke my brains out in the net, before making my way back out to the garage. The knot of guilt forms in my gut, and for a second I almost believe my own lie. Maybe I will hurl.

I keep dialing her number as I whip through downtown traffic. Watching for texts from Ronni or Elliot, someone, anyone. I need to get to my girl. Getting to her building, I don't even wait on the elevator, taking the stairs two at a time.

I knock on her door, and hear nothing from the other side. I pound louder, calling her name through the wood. I breathe in relief when I hear the locks move from her side, but my relief is short-lived when I see her. She looks wrecked. Her cheeks are damn, her eyes, red and puffy.

"Oh, Duchess," I murmur, stepping forward to pull her into a hug as she dissolves into sobs against my chest. "I'm so sorry."

"He had pictures. Someone followed me everywhere and he had pictures. He took ones of us at the club. They know–" Jess hiccups. "They know about us. They didn't even give me a chance to ex-explain," she stammers, sniffling into my neck.

"Hey, let's go inside and sit down." I slowly guide her inside, shutting the door and guiding her to the couch. Her laptop is open to job listings. "Who is 'he,' who had pictures?"

"HR. They said a 'concerned fan' sent them, but it had to be someone who is a club member, right?"

The anger that has been at a dull simmer in my chest, flares again. "They had pictures of us kissing outside the apartment, one of me in your lap in the club. What else did he see?" She sniffs, wiping at her eyes. "The crazy part is I'm not even mad about the job, I just feel violated."

I want to tell her she's not the only one. I want to tell her I can fix it and make it all go away, but I don't know how. "What else did HR tell you?"

"They said I was in breach of contract because of the nonfraternization clause, and they said something about a morality clause, but I don't even remember much of that. My head went fuzzy after I saw the pictures."

"It's okay, we can fix this." I glance at the laptop screen, the string of social media, managers, and marketing jobs and their locations. "Those are not in Rockville."

"The odds I will ever be able to work in this city again are slim tonight."

"Fuck that. You're working for me."

"No way. I am not gonna be a charity case. And I most certainly am not going to work under you while you're fucking me."

"Well, I need marketing, and you are the one that I trust. Besides, you wouldn't be working under me, it would be a partnership if anything."

"It's such a bad idea," she moans.

"It's the best idea I've ever had."

THE IMPOSSIBLE HAS HAPPENED. I don't even know how, but the thing I said would never ever occur, is here… I somehow managed to fall in love. This bratty social media manager has me wrapped around her finger and there's not a damn thing I can do about it, and I don't even think I want to escape.

Walking into the club tonight, seeing her stand at the same table I saw her at the first night, wearing those same ridiculous sky high heels? Hottest fucking thing that I've ever seen, ever. My beautiful, intelligent, headstrong woman, my Duchess. I would give her anything her heart desires. I would give her everything I am, and everything I own.

Everything I own.

The words rattle in my skull and I realize with clarity what I want.

Knowing she is here as my equal in every way. Going home with her every night.

Home. My heart clenches at the word.

. . .

She looks over at me, giving me the soft smile that absolutely unravels me, before looking back at the phone in front of her. I stop at the bar, gather our drinks and approach her just in time to catch her conversation with a floor manager.

"Numbers have doubled since you came on, Jess! This is magic!"

Setting the glasses on the table, I chime in, *"She's amazing."*

"All I did was post about a couple upcoming events, it wasn't that serious."

"Women have been applying at a much higher rate, and the reservations for the soft restraint workshop were off the charts! Seriously, I don't know how you do it." He excuses himself, heading toward the bar.

Jess blushes under the praise, and just looks toward me.

"Marry me." I freeze. The words hang between us, and I'm faintly aware that we're standing alone, just staring at each other.

"What…"

"Shit. I had a plan for this. This wasn't it. But damn it, I want you with me all the time."

"You're serious."

"Deadly. I want this more than anything. More than another Cup." Her wide eyes are locked on mine, bordering on panicked. "Come with me, let's talk in the office." Without another word I take her hand, nearly dragging her into my office, shutting the door behind us. Her face is still shell-shocked, her breaths a little shallow. "I'm sorry, I shouldn't have–"

"Yes."

"What?"

"Yes. Yes, oh my God." I can't even say who moved first, but she's in my arms, and peppering kisses across my face and–

"You said yes… We're…" Her laughter catches me off

guard, but my brain finally catches up with what is going on. She said yes. We're engaged. I– "Wait. I don't have a ring."

"Valentin Bishop, since when have we ever done anything in order?" She'spractically vibrating as she takes my jaw in her hands. "I love you," she whispers, before kissing me softly.

I try my damnedest to keep things light, but as she deepens the kiss, I ignite like wildfire. My hands drop to her thighs, hoisting her up so she can wrap her legs around me, and I carry her to my desk. Letting go of her with one hand, I swipe away the carefully stacked bills and notebooks, settling her on the edge of the desk.

"Mine," I growl, trailing kisses down her neck as she works to undo my pants.

"No. Mine," she counters, wrapping her hand around my cock. I groan, my knees nearly buckling at the contact. Within moments, I have her panties pulled to the side, and her wet heat wrapped around me. It's quick, messy, but neither one of us can see anything past just being together. I hear nothing past her breathy moans, the creak of the desk, and one consistent statement between us both—I love you.

I come so hard my vision goes black around the edges, but she's there, holding me together as we both come down. I press slow, lazy kisses, along her collarbone, up her throat, before looking at her fully blissed-out face.

"We'll never be able to tell people this proposal story," she murmurs with a giggle.

"We'll have a proper one later," I promise, kissing her again.

A knock at the door interrupts us.

"Hey B, when you're available we might have a problem out front."

I groan, dropping my forehead to Jess's as she giggles again. "He'll be out in a moment," she answers. We share a wicked grin, and she straightens our clothing. I can't stop myself from leaning down to kiss her again. "You're not helping."

"Sure I am, we're not done yet," I respond.

"Work first. Then play." She bites her lip as she takes in my loosened hair and wrinkled shirt. "But maybe we can come back here after we figure out what's going on."

"Deal." I smooth down her skirt over her thighs. "It's so fucking hot to see you work."

"I know. Why do you think I'm here?" She winks mischievously, dodging my grabbing hands and dashes to the door. "Are you going out in public like that, or do you need a moment?"

Working with my soon-to-be wife was the best worst decision I have ever made.

The End

EPILOGUE

Two Years Later

THE DEEP BASS thrums through me as I look out across our club, watching our guests enjoy the night. Low lights pulse in time with the beat, illuminating a sea of bodies that meet, caress, tease, and move away, to repeat the cycle again. I love this little space that we have created together. The balcony view from our executive office is my favorite,

I shift my gaze down to the bar, to my husband–*my fucking husband!* My heart flutters watching him interact with our guests. My heart pounds as I admire him, his impeccably tailored suit hugging his muscles, his dark hair pulled back in his signature ponytail, the streaks of silver taking on the colors of the lights. I love that he hasn't tried to dye them away, especially now as a retired player.

Leaving hockey behind was hard for both of us, in the beginning, first with my shift out of the PR team, and then with his retirement the following season. Adjusting to being "home" all the time was a new concept for him, after so many seasons of away games. With the growth in Caissa, both from the front of house and VIP in the back, we've found an energy outlet so he doesn't miss the sport that he loved for so many years.

My phone buzzes in my hand, the light making my engagement ring sparkle. I glance down and smile, seeing the text notification across the screen.

> Bishop: Are you going to stay up there staring at me all night, or do I get to have my beautiful wife on my arm?

I smirk down at the handsome man gazing back at me, curling two fingers to motion me down to him. I blow him a kiss and turn away, passing back through the doors to journey down to the main floor, and to him. The man I love

Passing the hallway of private rooms, I hear men's voices, and a woman's moan. While not completely out of place to hear, it shouldn't be that audible back here. Soft lighting glows from a cracked door, so I wander that way to close it for my guests. A small courtesy in case the open door was unplanned voyeurism.

"That's our girl, *kotya*, make a mess on him," a male voice demands. The accent sounds familiar, but I can't place it exactly.

"Fuck, I'm not going to last if you keep that up, Koz."

I freeze. I know that voice, and that nickname. I'm not totally surprised that Robicheaux is here, I know he's a member, but playing with Kozlov? In the club?

"You're going to last because she comes first, damn it," Kozlov growls. "Fuck, Bridge, so good,' he croons.

Kozlov is talking to Bridgette? There's only one I know of that Roby knows, her dad owns the team.

"Holy shit," I whisper to myself, pulling the door closed softly and scurrying down the hall before anyone can see me.

ACKNOWLEDGMENTS

Bishop took a little longer to come together, but I'm grateful for everyone who stayed on for the journey.

Rose, of course, for knocking the new covers out of the park. So pretty! The pretty pastels all in a row look perfect for the series. Thank you for taking "I don't know, make them more to market" and making it happen! Early reactions to Tripping and Fighting give me

The Romance Riot, Cincinnati Author Coven, and Hype Girls all had my back for the ride! I'm so grateful for my group chats and support systems, and how we're always there for each other. Being an author is a tireless job at the end of the day, and having friends around who are in the same trenches with you makes a huge difference. Knowing that someone is just a text away to hear the unhinged "hear me out…" thoughts before I commit them to paper means everything. Writing isn't a competition, it's a collaboration.

My friends and family, the ones who use either title interchangeably. Here we are, three books in and you haven't gotten scared off yet. I used to start the dedications off with what chapters to skip in order to keep things from getting awkward at special occasions, but since I know you just skip to those spots like it's a road map…you're on your own, haha. No, seriously, thank you for all of the support, it means the world to me.

Paige, who spent a decent chunk of a six-hour road trip home from a book signing riffing back and forth with me about Bishop and his adventure in love. He wouldn't be the

Cinna-Dom Daddy with a breeding kink without you! Thank you, babes!!

Irene, of course, who saw Bishop in his rawest, dirtiest form and helped me polish him up. Thank you for hearing me out and talking me through the bouts of author panic when things got rough, and I couldn't get the words out. Also, thank you for not letting me rely on just pretty with him — I mean, he is pretty, but he has so much more to him than that. Viv and Woody also thank you for demanding justice for their story, and I'm honestly excited to get into their project! They're totally next!

My readers. I couldn't do any of this without you, honestly. Well, I could, but it would be boring and I would spend all my time looking at Word documents going, "That's trash, I'm trash, I'm never doing that again!" You keep me on track, and determined to give you the Ice Wolves stories you want and deserve. Thank you so much for your commitment and I hope you continue to stay on the journey.

WOODY

Butterflies take flight in my stomach as I stand in the elevator, pressing myself into the corner behind a giant, gaudy looking stuffed unicorn that had to be the size of an average adult. Lugging it down the sidewalk, hearing people curse as they tried to avoid me lurching blindly in the middle of the path, should have definitely counted as my cardio for the day. Bishop can't be too mad at me for that., right?

But here I am, on my way to her apartment with this ridiculous gift, to show that I am serious and shoot my shot with someone who is by far the prettiest person I've ever seen.

The ding of the elevator alerts me to the door opening, and I can just make out the "5" in the red digital display over the top of the silver doors. This was it, she said this was her building, and her floor.

Had I ever been to her place before? No.

Did she invite me up today? No.

Did I hope she would be surprised? Absolutely!

My shoes squeak on the battered linoleum, and I try to

peek around the neck of this giant thing at the gold plated numbers on the doors.

This is it, I think, looking at the 513 on the door. Reaching out blindly, I rap my knuckles against the wood and stand back, waiting patiently. I can hear footsteps on the other side of the door, and a muffled curse before the lock clicks.

"Can I help you?"

I jolt at the man's voice. A man? She didn't say her roomate was a guy, or maybe I missed it.

"Hey, um, I was looking for Andrea. Is she here?"

"No, she's out on a…wait, what's your name?"

"Woody. Oh, is she still at work? I can go meet her there—"

"Oh, buddy, you might want to come in…" he cringes. "I'm Adam, by the way."

"Nice to meet you. I don't remember her saying she had a roommate."

Adam pauses, looking at me standing in the hallway.

"I'm not her roommate, Woody. I'm her boyfriend. I take it she didn't tell you…figures. Come in, least I can do is offer you a beer after you lugged this thing across town."

I don't mention to him that I'm not even legal yet, not until next month. The guys have been kicking my ass over the fact that I probably will still be underage if we win the cup in a few weeks. Having this week off before the finals helps get me closer to my 21st birthday, but I have never had the play-offs go that long.

I should go. Leave this with him and leave. Or just leave and drop this randomly somewhere because what the hell will I do with this. However, he offered, and it would be rude to turn him down, so I shove the pink and purple unicorn through the open doorway, allowing the door to close behind me.

I set the stuffed monstrosity in an armchair, gritting my teeth in frustration as the head flops and it drifts off-balance, nearly falling to the floor. I move it to the couch instead, pressing it in between the arm and myself as I sit on the leather cushion. Maybe Adam will sit over in the abandonned armchair instead.

"Here, take this," he says, holding out a bottle starting to sweat in the early June humidity.

"Thanks. Sorry about dropping in on you like this." I cringe as the words fall out of my mouth, almost with a mind of their own. Shut the hell up, I hiss at myself, physically cringing at myself. I can hear Bishop in my head. Stop apologizing so damn much. Your job is too be a brick wall, by any means. Never apologize for denying someone their goal.

My gaze drops to the clear bottle, and I feel panic bubble up in my chest. What am I doing? I should be running away, hiding, anything but having a beer with a giant stuffed unicorn and the boyfriend of the girl I...like? I watch him sip his, and I do the same, holding back a grimace at the taste. Okay, maybe I'm not a beer guy. I can still fake this.

"So, how did you meet?" Adam's question is soft, not forceful. Curious sounding, if anything.

"We ran into each other at the bookstore on 9th," I reply, taking another sip. "We were both reaching for the newest book in The Ravendale Series." I keep the detail of letting her keep the book in my favorite fantasy series to myself, I don't need him laughing because I'm a nerd.

"Good book, I remember her coming home with it. She said it was the last one."

"Yeah, I'm still waiting on the store to call with my copy."

"Hang tight, Woody." He gets up, walking over to a set of bookshelves. He wraps a hand around the spine of the same book, bringing it over to me. "Here. We ended up with duplicate copies because I also got one the same day."

"I couldn't..." I start to say, shame blanketing the panic I felt.

"It's the least I can do. I don't think she explained our situation very well, and I'd like to try to fix it."

"Situation?" I can't be that drunk, I should still be able to understand how words work.

"We're in an open relationship. And sometimes we share. But something tells me that she didn't let you know any of that beforehand."

"I don't know what any of that means." I cringe as my voice cracks. God I sound like such a baby.

Adam sighs, turning toward me slightly on the cushion. "We're together, but sometimes we like other people. And sometimes we explore those feelings with these other people alone, but sometimes we entertain them…together." The word hangs heavy between us, his eyes never leaving mine like he's waiting for me to… *oh.*

"Oh, you mean…" he nods in a silent answer. "I don't know if that's something I can do. You're great and all, but…" There is no way in hell I'm explaining to this guy that I don't know if 'sharing' is something I can do because I've never even *had* a traditional relationship before, let alone one with more than one person. I set the half-empty beer on the coaster, and move to stand. "I'm going to go. Thanks for the beer, and I hope you two are happy. Um, she can still have that," I nod awkwardly at the slumping unicorn.

"Understandable. Be safe out there, and good luck in the finals, okay?"

With a nod, I shuffle towards the door, mortified that not only am I getting rejected, but that he also knows who the hell I really am.

I'm the rookie goalie of the Ice Wolves who is still a freaking virgin and apparently a failure at shooting his shot.

HOME ICE ADVANTAGE

ELLIE

Sometimes, coming to a home game feels like going back in time. I swear to God, if I get offered another non-alcoholic beverage while being talked to like I'm a 12-year-old again, I'm going to fucking scream.

I should feel like I belong in the family box on home ice. I've watched games here since they hired my dad to coach the Ice Wolves a decade ago. The head office staff have known me for the majority of my life. Instead, I feel infantilized. I've been out of college for an entire year. I guess it's to be expected growing up in this arena, honestly. I'm in my twenties, I'm a fucking legal adult, but they still treat me like I'm that gangly kid trailing behind her daddy.

I haven't been that girl in a long, long time.

My phone buzzes in my hand, and I sigh in relief as I see my best friend's name flash across the screen, obscuring our graduation photo together. She's my ride or die, my "if we aren't married to anyone before we turn thirty, we're getting a Golden Girls bungalow together."

"Girl, where the hell are you? I thought you were coming

to the game with me!" Kimmy and I are light years beyond social niceties.

"Sorry, babe, my mom needed me for a photo op. Some children's charity event or something. I'll hang with you after?"

"Damn it. That sucks, I miss you," I grumble, looking at the Jumbotron to calculate how much longer until I'd see her again. "I swear, if I get offered another vodka soda without the vodka again with a wink, I'm going to lose it," I whisper into my phone, eyeballing the stakeholder who did just that earlier with some off-the-cuff comment about it being a school night, of all things. The tone echoed in my head, he liked the idea of school nights a bit too much. Maybe he's into the school girl thing, but that's not my jam.

After we end the call, I wander to the edge of the family space, looking down at the ice. The first period is well under-way, and the Ice Wolves look solid this year, all high on the power play from a quick fight. It's just another Saturday night – I've been here hundreds of times.

I shift my gaze around at the stands to the proud fans sporting jerseys and Ice Wolves hoodies, cheering loudly. People-watching has always entertained me. It's also given me ideas for my upcoming marketing internships. Watching the fans interact with the various hype events during commercial breaks gives me ideas on what to suggest in the future. Sneaking a peek at the neighboring boxes, it's curious how different the lower bowl fan base reacts to the game, versus the luxury boxes. I pause, my observation falling on the box to my right.

At first glance, it looks like a group of older tech bros. Middle aged men in a uniform of polo shirts and khakis, high fiving each other with one hand while holding pale beers or rocks glasses in the other. While the self-congratulatory group chats amongst themselves, one man sits to the side by himself.

His dark hair has streaks of silver through it, and there's the faintest hint of shadow along his sharp jawline. He seems taller than the rest, and his white button down and dark slacks stand out against the sea of khakis and polos.

A silver fox, in the wild. Color me impressed.

Older men have always been more attractive to me than guys my own age. Maybe it's their maturity, or the ability to think past their own wants and needs. A rebellious thought hit me, and I can't help but let the daydream grow: What if the silver fox in the box beside me was like Daddy? A sliver of guilt passes through me. I don't know his name or what he looks like, just the screen name of Daddy.

I quickly swipe on the phone before I can talk myself out of it. Camera on, I take a series of photos and short videos, capturing my best angles. Some light edits later, and then I'm uploading to my secret subscription site.

And now I wait.

JACK

I don't know why I let my office talk me into this. Sure, I like hockey, but this wasn't how I wanted to spend my Saturday night. Not that I had a ton of say in the matter. Rubbing elbows and getting my name out there is all that all matters. Networking has to come before anything else until the election, and it will probably get worse after that.

Mindlessly scrolling on my phone while my top donors are distracted, I try to ignore the avalanche of notifications popping up. Requests for interviews, another text rescheduling dinner with my daughter, and…

What's this?

IcePrincess has posted a new image.

Well, this is an interesting turn of events.

I glance around, making sure that no one is paying attention to me. With a quick swipe, I have the app open and there she is – my Princess.

At my age, maybe I should be ashamed of using an app like this. Paying for a subscription for photos of half-naked women – more specifically, this half-naked goddess – probably would destroy my career aspirations, but the risk is worth the reward.

Especially with the photo she just posted.

It isn't even overly sexy or revealing, but that tease of skin makes my heart pound. A pic shot from above, aimed into her ample cleavage, framed by a blue Ice Wolves varsity jacket.

Yeah, I'd recognize those tits anywhere.

As I've done for months now, I open up the app to leave her a large tip.

I'd give her a large tip, alright.

Jesus, quit thinking like a caveman.

It grants me access to a chat window to see her message pop up first.

> IcePrincess: Thank you, Daddy.

> Me: Is my pretty little princess enjoying showing off in public?

> IcePrincess: Just for you.

> Me: Show me how short that skirt is.

I look back out toward the game as the home team scores again, taking it to 4-0. It's just a preseason game, but the imbalance makes the night boring. My phone hums against my palm; at least someone is keeping me entertained.

A new private video posted for you.

I smirk as the words flash on my screen. I take a quick

glance to make sure the few people left in my box aren't paying attention, and open the app again. Her legs are crossed, only a hint of thigh showing, and then she moves. The angle changes slightly as her legs uncross, thighs parting and lifting the skirt higher, before recrossing again. Black knee high boots and bare thighs are my absolute weakness. It's a ridiculous thought, but fantasizing that she wears it just for me, drives me crazy.

What piques my interest even more than the absolute perfection she has on display, is the background—a luxury box identical to mine.

She's here.

I scan the boxes near me, seeking out a flash of her jacket among the sea of hockey sweaters. Adrenaline courses through my veins as I consider how close we are. What are the odds that I could see her in person or…touch her?

Oh, what I would give to touch her.

My eyes catch on a curvy brunette sitting in the box to my left. She's sitting by herself, scrunched low in the seats, the rest of the box full of people behind her.

Is that her?

I fire off a flirty message, keeping it light.

> Me: Showing off your pretty thighs in public. The things I would do to you…

> IcePrincess: Too bad you're not. What would you do, Daddy?

I choose my next words carefully. This can either go so right, or so wrong. I hold my breath and push send.

> Me: Who says I'm not?

> IcePrincess: I don't believe you.

Oh, sweet girl, you have no idea what you've just done. My fingers fly across my screen in response.

> Me: I should warm that fine ass of yours for that, Princess. However, since you insist....

I snap a picture of the scoreboard, attaching it to the text.

Her thumbs hover over the screen. Fuck, I said too much, she's going to call for security any moment now. She freezes, her wide eyes locked on her screen, teeth pressing into her bottom lip.

And then she types.

> IcePrincess: You're really at the game too, Daddy?

———

Find out more about Ellie's experience with the silver fox in "On the Breakaway," available now.

ALSO BY EDEN KNOX

Tripping for Number 68

Fighting for Number 57

On the Breakaway: Short Stories From The Sin Bin

Ebooks are available on Kindle Unlimited. Paperbacks are available everywhere paperbacks are sold online.

For personalized signed copies, visit www.edenknoxauthor.com

ABOUT THE AUTHOR

Eden Knox is a sports romance author who lives in Ohio with her 2 girls, herd of animals, and her retired veteran husband. When she isn't screaming at hockey or football games, she's working on tormenting her fictional hockey team or completing coursework for grad school.

instagram.com/edenknoxwrites
facebook.com/eden.knox.145432